OBAN - 8/18

C000186092

15 SEP 2017

ROT

ARGYLL AND BUTE COUNCIL
LIBRARY AND INFORMATION SERVICE

Books should be returned on or before the date above.
Renewals may be made in person, by telephone,
or on-line if not in demand.
Visit www.argyll-bute.gov.uk/libraries

RESCUING
DR MacALLISTER

BY
SARAH MORGAN

ROT

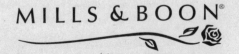

DID YOU PURCHASE THIS BOOK WITHOUT A COVER?

If you did, you should be aware it is **stolen property** as it was reported *unsold and destroyed* by a retailer. Neither the author nor the publisher has received any payment for this book.

All the characters in this book have no existence outside the imagination of the author, and have no relation whatsoever to anyone bearing the same name or names. They are not even distantly inspired by any individual known or unknown to the author, and all the incidents are pure invention.

All Rights Reserved including the right of reproduction in whole or in part in any form. This edition is published by arrangement with Harlequin Enterprises II B.V. The text of this publication or any part thereof may not be reproduced or transmitted in any form or by any means, electronic or mechanical, including photocopying, recording, storage in an information retrieval system, or otherwise, without the written permission of the publisher.

This book is sold subject to the condition that it shall not, by way of trade or otherwise, be lent, resold, hired out or otherwise circulated without the prior consent of the publisher in any form of binding or cover other than that in which it is published and without a similar condition including this condition being imposed on the subsequent purchaser.

MILLS & BOON and MILLS & BOON with the Rose Device are registered trademarks of the publisher.

First published in Great Britain 2003
Harlequin Mills & Boon Limited,
Eton House, 18-24 Paradise Road, Richmond, Surrey TW9 1SR

© Sarah Morgan 2003

ISBN 0 263 83444 1

Set in Times Roman 10½ on 11½ pt.
03-0503-48742

Printed and bound in Spain
by Litografia Rosés, S.A., Barcelona

PROLOGUE

HE HATED hospitals.

Ben MacAllister stared at the bold red sign for the Accident and Emergency unit and wondered what on earth had possessed him to take the job. It had been a moment of weakness and one which he was already bitterly regretting.

What the hell had he been thinking of?

He could have stayed in the clinic in Pakistan where they were desperate for doctors with his skills, or he could have done what he'd been promising himself for ages and taken a year off and travelled.

In fact, he'd had any number of options, all of which were considerably more appealing than the one that he'd chosen.

With an impatient sigh, he strode across the car park to the entrance. If he didn't get himself inside the building soon he'd be climbing back into the car and driving back the way he'd come.

Forcing himself to move, he strode through the swing doors and stopped dead as the memories came rushing back. The smells, the noise, the bustle…

That one awful day that had changed his life.

Sweat broke out on his brow and he gritted his teeth to stop himself running.

This was never going to work.

He was about to turn and go back the way he'd come when his oldest friend came striding through the swing doors towards him, stethoscope looped round his neck like a tame serpent.

5

'Ben—great to see you!'

'Nicholson.' He clasped the hand that was offered, aware that his brief chance for escape had vanished. 'How are you?'

'Relieved to see you.' Sean Nicholson shot a telling glance towards the crowded waiting room. 'Where do they all come from? I'm trying to run this department with zero staff at the moment so you're as welcome as alcohol on a stag night. Let's go to my office and talk.'

Ben reluctantly kept pace as the other man led him down the corridor into a small office which overlooked the car park and the mountains beyond.

Sean waved a hand at a chair buried under a mound of papers. 'Move those files and sit down.'

'I'd rather stand.' Ben paced over to the window and stared outside, feeling some of the tension in his body dissipate as he stared at the snow-capped mountains. It always soothed him to be in the mountains. It was a reminder that there was a world outside if things got too bad within the hospital. 'Nice view.'

Sean smiled. 'Being the senior consultant comes with some perks. It's not the Himalayas, but we like it.' His smile faded. 'You stayed away too long. You look like hell, MacAllister.'

'Thanks.' He should have been offended by Sean's blunt comment, but he wasn't. After all, it was true. He *did* look like hell.

And he didn't want to be here. It wasn't going to work.

Sean's voice was rough but there was sympathy in his blue eyes. 'You needed to come back, Ben, and you know it.'

'Is that what this is all about? Rehabilitation?' Ben's tone was weary and his mouth tightened. 'When you called, you told me that you were desperate for doctors.'

'I am desperate,' Sean said calmly. 'You have no idea

just how desperate I am. I'm trying to run a department on fresh air at the moment. Having you here helps alleviate the problem and it makes my wife feel better.'

The expression in Ben's eyes softened slightly at the mention of Sean's wife. 'How is Ally?'

'Worried about you,' Sean said frankly. 'She wants you close by so that she can help.'

Ben's expression was unreadable. 'So basically you're interfering?'

'Well, it's time someone did.' Sean met his accusing gaze head on. 'It's been two years, Ben.'

'And what's that supposed to mean?' Ben's eyes glittered dangerously. 'Is two years some sort of magic figure? Am I supposed to feel better just because it's been two years?'

Sean sighed. 'No. But it's time you stopped running.' He hesitated. 'And maybe it's time you talked about what happened.'

'Why the hell would I want to do that?'

Sean looked him in the eye. 'Because sometimes it helps to talk?'

Ben threw back his head and laughed. 'That's rich, coming from you! When have you ever talked about your feelings?'

Sean rubbed the back of his neck awkwardly. 'I talk to Ally.'

Ben lifted an eyebrow. 'You're offering to lend me your wife?'

'I'm offering to lend you her listening skills. Ally wants you to come and spend some time with us.'

Ben's mouth tightened. 'You can tell Ally not to meddle.' But he knew she meant well. He was very fond of Sean's wife who was mature and sensible and knew exactly what she wanted out of life.

Unlike some women.

'You can tell her yourself,' Sean said crisply. 'She wants you to come to dinner as soon as you're settled in.'

Ben digested this information. 'Don't tell me—she's inviting a spare woman?'

Sean fiddled with some papers on his desk and avoided eye contact. 'I'm not involved with the guest list. I just turn up and eat the food.'

'Sean!' Ben's tone held a warning note and Sean sighed and raked a hand through his hair.

'All right, there's a possibility that she's matchmaking...'

'Possibility?'

Sean shifted uncomfortably. 'Probability. You know Ally.' He gave a shrug. 'It doesn't mean anything.'

Ben gritted his teeth. He had no intention of being set up. 'Forget it.'

Sean sighed. 'It's only dinner! Dinner, and one available woman to talk to. It's not as if you hate women—or are you trying to tell me that you've been celibate for the past two years?'

Ben chose to ignore that question.

'I'm not interested.'

'Oh, come on!' Sean gave a disbelieving look. 'I knew you in medical school remember? Women get cricked necks when you pass them in the street. You had more girlfriends than—'

'That was a long time ago.' Ben interrupted him with a grim expression on his face. 'Things have changed.'

He'd changed.

Sean's look spoke volumes. 'You're seriously trying to tell me that you haven't been with a woman for two years?'

Ben's dark brows settled into an ominous frown. 'What business is that of yours?'

'I'm your friend,' Sean reminded him, 'and I want to

see you get your life back together. Maybe it would help to meet a decent woman and—'

'Sean, listen to me.' Ben's voice was tired. 'I know you think women solve everything, but in my case you're wrong. My life is fine and I'm certainly not a good deal for any decent woman.'

Sean looked genuinely bemused. 'Well, why the hell not? According to Ally, you're stunningly good-looking—' He broke off as he considered the implications of what he'd just said. 'I grilled her over that, by the way. I'm not at all keen on the fact my wife freely admits to finding you irresistible.' He shook himself slightly. 'Anyway, that aside, apparently you're the original macho action man and women love that, you've got money, you—'

'I never realised you felt this way about me.' Ben's tone was dry and his friend waved a hand.

'Relax. I prefer blondes. You're not my type.'

Ben gave a short laugh. 'I'm not anybody's type. Not if they've got any sense. I don't have anything to offer anyone. I'm not claiming to have lived like a monk, but I can honestly say that I haven't felt anything for a woman for two years.'

And he doubted whether he'd ever feel anything again. It was as if he was dead inside. Even the few flings he'd had hadn't really worked for him. Usually because the woman he was with so obviously wanted more than he was able to give.

Which was nothing more than brief physical satisfaction.

Sean looked at him. 'Give it time. It's grief that makes you feel that way.'

Grief?

Sean made it sound so simple, but Ben knew that it was so much more than grief that had locked his emotions inside himself. It was anger, too. Anger and bitterness and guilt.

Oh, yes, definitely guilt.

But Sean didn't know any of that, of course, and why should he? Ben wasn't in the habit of discussing his feelings with anyone. What was the point? It wouldn't change what had happened.

And as for giving it time—well, it had been two years already. He'd given it more than enough time and nothing had changed. He still felt the same way as he had when it had first happened. As far as he was concerned, time had healed nothing.

'How was Pakistan?' Sean changed the subject neatly and Ben accepted the change readily.

'Interesting. Challenging. Hard work.'

'Good.' Sean nodded briskly. 'A bit like the job here, then.'

The job.

Ben opened his mouth to say that he didn't think he could do it but the words didn't come out the way he'd planned. 'So when do you want me to start?'

He listened to himself and almost laughed.

What was he saying? Was he crazy?

He didn't want to start at all. He wanted to turn around and walk out of the department the way he'd come without bothering to look back. Not submit himself to torture.

On the other hand, maybe it was time to face his demons.

'You saw the waiting room. How about now?' Sean gave a wry smile and fingered the stethoscope around his neck. 'Only joking. The day after tomorrow will do fine. That should give you time to settle into the place I've found for you to live. It's great. You'll love it.' He reached into his drawer and pulled out a set of keys and a map. 'A log cabin in a forest. It's easy enough to find but watch the roads. The weather has been filthy for almost twenty-four hours and there's no sign of it letting up. Some of the roads are flooded and there are trees down, so go easy.'

Ben glanced out of the window. 'After some of the roads in Pakistan—or rather the lack of them—I can cope with the Lake District. But I'm in no hurry, Sean. Why don't you show me round while I'm here and then I can get straight on with it the day after tomorrow?'

'You're not dying to go and clean up?'

Ben rubbed long fingers over his roughened jaw and lifted an eyebrow. 'Am I that bad?'

Sean looked him over. 'Let's just say I can tell you've been in the wilds for the last year. You're what Ally would call rugged.' He stood up and walked towards the door. 'Do me a favour and lose the designer stubble and some of your hair before you start or the hospital management will be complaining.'

Irritated by what he saw as a complete irrelevance, Ben's face darkened. 'I thought you took me on for my medical skills, not my appearance.'

Sean held the door open for him to pass. 'I did. But the way you look at the moment you'll scare the patients.' He gave a wicked smile and locked the door behind them. 'Unless they're female. You'll also distract my nurses and they're too busy for that. I want their minds on work, not sex.'

Ben shot him an exasperated look. 'Why did I ever agree to help you out?'

Sean slapped him on the shoulder as they walked into the corridor. 'Because I'm your best mate and you'd never let me down.'

Ben shook his head. 'Because I'm an idiot.' He stopped dead and stared at his friend. 'I can't promise you that this will work—you know that, don't you?'

Sean hesitated and then nodded reluctantly. 'Just promise me you'll give it a few months at least.'

A few months?

Ben felt sick at the thought. At the moment he doubted his ability to get through the next few minutes, let alone a few months.

He should never have taken the job.

CHAPTER ONE

IT WAS a filthy night and the river was flooded.

Ellie stopped the car and stared in dismay at the murky dark water swirling directly in her path, illuminated by the beam of her headlights. In the summer months the river flowed obediently under the road, but in the winter, particularly after torrential rain, it swelled and burst its banks, flooding the road and forcing drivers to make a long detour through another valley.

But she didn't have time for any sort of detour.

Lindsay was in labour. On her own and terrified in a farmhouse that was in the middle of nowhere.

Ellie flicked her windscreen wipers onto double speed and weighed up her options.

Turn around and approach Lindsay's farm from the other side of the valley?

No. She dismissed the thought instantly. It would take too much time and time was the one thing she didn't have.

Which left only one other option.

She narrowed her eyes and stared through the darkness at the swirling water.

'Oh, for goodness' sake, Lindsay!' She glared at the surging river as if sheer will-power could make the waters part like the Red Sea. 'Why did you have to buy a house in such a remote place? What was wrong with a nice stone cottage in the middle of Ambleside?'

Apparently the midwife had been very relaxed and reassuring on the phone, reminding her that the baby wasn't due for another four weeks and that the tightenings that Lindsay was feeling were probably normal.

13

Ellie peered at the swirling water and hoped the midwife knew what she was talking about. If she was wrong, Ellie would have to deliver the baby by herself, a challenge which she didn't relish. She was an A and E nurse, not a midwife.

In fact, if it hadn't been for Lindsay's cry for help, Ellie would have gone back to work because you didn't need to be a genius to know that the A and E department was going to be packed with injuries on a night like this.

Opening the car door, she flinched as a gust of wind tore it out of her hand and the rain flung itself in her face like water from a bucket.

'Ugh…' Gasping and scrubbing the water away from her eyes with her hand, she forced the car door shut and picked her way down to the edge of the water. Within minutes she was soaked, the pelting rain turning her long dark hair as sleek as an otter's, her dark lashes clogging together as she tried to see through the darkness.

How deep could it be?

She'd driven this way only the day before and the road had been clear. It had been raining for twenty-four hours but surely the water level couldn't have risen that fast?

The secret was to drive quickly and not hesitate.

She'd done it before in her youth, she reminded herself. Plenty of times.

Her mind made up, she hurried back to the car and scraped a hank of sodden hair away from her face.

Now that she'd made her decision, her eyes gleamed with anticipation and she started the engine, set her jaw and pressed the accelerator to the floor.

As she hit the water the car jerked and for one terrifying, breath-stealing moment she thought she was going to be stranded in the middle of the roaring river. And then she heard the engine splutter and the car suddenly surged forward and bounded out the other side as if it was relieved to be clear of the water.

She gave a whoop of triumph which turned to a groan as the car gave another splutter, choked and then stopped.

'Oh, no—don't do this to me.' She turned the key again but there was no response.

Her little car might have made it through the ford but there was no way it was going any further. She flopped back in her seat and stared out of the windscreen in dismay.

Now what?

All her thoughts were on Lindsay, alone, afraid and possibly in labour less than a mile away.

Lindsay—not just her cousin but her best friend.

There was no way anything was going to stop her reaching her.

Which meant she was going to have to walk the rest of the way.

But at least now she was on the right side of the water. She'd just have to leave the car where it was and sort it out later.

Reaching into the back of her car for her coat, she dragged it on, grabbed her bag and opened the car door again, bracing herself as she confronted the elements.

If anything the rain had increased and in seconds she was drenched to the skin, her vision distorted by the volume of water streaming over her face. The wind was so fierce she could hardly stand, let alone make headway up the road, and she swore under her breath as she battled to stay upright.

She'd barely made any progress when she heard the unmistakable sound of a car engine from behind her. Turning quickly, she saw headlights flickering in the darkness as another car made its way towards the ford.

For a moment she tensed. The water was deeper than it

looked, but there was no way of warning the driver. She just hoped he wouldn't suffer the same fate that she had.

He didn't.

Ellie watched enviously as the car surged through the water without any alteration in speed and then leapt out the other side as if it had barely noticed the impediment. Great. What wouldn't she have given for a car like that on a night like this?

Still, she might be able to make use of it.

Ignoring the fact that the wind was trying to tear her coat from her shoulders, she braced her legs apart, stood in the middle of the road and windmilled her arms.

Oh, please, please, let the driver stop.

If the driver could drop her at the end of Lindsay's lane, she'd save precious time.

The car pulled up and there was a soft purr as the window on the passenger side slid down.

The wind whipped her sodden hair across her face and she raked it to one side impatiently as she leaned inside to talk to the driver.

'Thank goodness you stopped!' She was shouting to make herself heard above the wind. 'I need a lift, it's an emergency.'

Without waiting for an invitation, she yanked open the door and clambered into the passenger seat, giving an exclamation of disgust as the wind tried to drag the door from her hand.

With considerable difficulty she slammed it shut, closed the electric window and turned to the driver with a relieved smile.

'What a night! Thank goodness you came along when you did. I was in a spot of bother.'

There was an ominous silence and in the darkness the driver's features were barely visible. When he finally spoke, his voice had a hard edge. 'Do you have a death wish?'

The temperature inside the car suddenly seemed lower than outside, and Ellie's merry smile faltered slightly as she looked into glittering black eyes.

'Of course I don't have a death wish.'

'You took an absurd risk.'

'By driving through the ford?' She gave a chuckle and toed off her wet shoes. 'I hate to point out the obvious, but you drove through it, too!'

'In a vehicle designed for those sorts of conditions,' he growled. 'The same can't be said for your car.'

'Wasn't she amazing?' Ellie squinted through clogged lashes towards her little car, her tone warm with affection. 'I mean, I know she conked out on me but at least she made it through the water.'

'You could have been killed.'

'Relax, will you?' She smiled cheerfully as she peeled off her soaking wet coat and pulled her sodden jumper over her head. 'I've got nine lives.'

'Not any more.' His voice was clipped. 'You just lost at least three back there in the river.'

Why was he so angry?

'I've been driving through that ford since I was young, although admittedly I haven't done it for a while now. There was no danger.'

She dropped her wet clothes onto the floor of the car and tugged her wet shirt out of her trousers.

'Are you planning to remove all your clothes?'

'Just the outer layers,' she assured him. 'I'm soaked to the skin and I don't want to get hypothermia. What I really need is a towel. I don't suppose…?' Her voice trailed off as she saw the expression in his eyes. 'No, you're not the type to carry a towel in the car.'

He seemed to struggle to find his voice. 'I don't generally need towels when I drive,' he said finally, and she rubbed her arms to keep warm.

'Well, you should,' she told him. 'They can be very useful. I remember one time when I was driving home from work, I passed this injured sheep—'

He blinked in disbelief. 'Sheep?'

'Yes, *sheep*.' She gave him an odd look and then shrugged and carried on. 'Anyway, she'd managed to wriggle her way under the barbed-wire fence and she was totally wedged and every time she moved the wire embedded itself deeper in her wool and—why are you looking at me like that?'

'I've never met anyone that talks as much as you. I'm wondering when you breathe.'

'I can breathe and talk,' she assured him. 'As I was saying, she was stuck, and I've tried rescuing sheep with bare hands before and it's always been a disaster, but luckily I had a towel in my car and so I used that and it was brilliant. I always carry one now. You should too.'

He stared at her for a long time and then finally stirred and cleared his throat. 'I'll remember that. In the meantime, I do have a blanket on the back seat. Please feel free to use it.'

'Oh, thanks.' Completely unselfconscious, Ellie reached into the back, grabbed the blanket and then shook herself like a drenched kitten. Droplets of water flew from her dark hair and landed on the driver. 'Gosh, I'm soaked and freezing. Can we turn your heating up?'

'Be my guest.'

She glanced at him warily as she fiddled with the controls of his fancy car.

'You're looking at me in a funny way. I suppose you think I'm very forward, but I'm sure you wouldn't want me to get hypothermia. I remember once when I got really wet—'

'Do you always talk this much?'

'Are you always this tense?' She peered at him, trying to read his expression in the semi-darkness. 'Have I made you late or something? It was very kind of you to stop.'

'You were standing in the middle of the road,' he reminded her with exaggerated patience. 'I had no choice but to stop. It was that or run you over.'

'If you're trying to convince me that given the choice you would have driven past me and left me there, you won't succeed,' she said cheerfully. 'No one would be that heartless.'

There was a long pause and when he finally spoke his tone was chilly. 'You have a worrying faith in human nature.'

She frowned. 'No, I haven't. Most people are very kind-hearted. Like you. I don't know what I would have done if you hadn't come along when you did. You're my knight in shining armour and I'll love you forever.' She snuggled under the blanket and gave him a wide smile which faltered when she saw the look on his face. 'What? Why are you looking at me like that? What have I done now?'

In the gloom his expression was hard to read but she sensed his exasperation.

'Are you always this reckless?'

'Reckless?' She subdued a yawn and snuggled deeper under the blanket. 'When was I reckless?'

'When?' He lifted one dark eyebrow and his expression was ironic. 'Well, let's see—was it when you drove the ford in a car no bigger than a sewing machine, or flagged down a total stranger, climbed into his car, stripped off your clothes and declared undying love—'

'Not undying love exactly,' Ellie corrected him with a quick frown. 'More eternal thanks.'

He gritted his teeth. 'You're not safe to be let out alone.

Didn't your father teach you never to accept lifts from strange men?'

For a brief moment Ellie's smile faltered. 'Yes,' she said in a small voice, 'I suppose he did.'

'So what were you doing, flagging down a total stranger?'

'Well, it was that or die of exposure,' Ellie said logically, pushing away thoughts of her beloved father. 'Dad may have taught me not to accept lifts from strange men, but he also taught me to use my head in a crisis. And tonight is definitely a crisis.'

'I could be anyone.' His voice had a hard edge, but Ellie just smiled trustingly and snuggled further under the blanket.

'I'm sure you're a lovely person. In my experience, most people are.'

'Then you obviously haven't had much experience,' he said roughly. 'How old are you?'

He flicked on the internal light and she blinked.

'You shouldn't ask a woman her age. It isn't polite. And you shouldn't be influenced by appearances.' Ellie's voice tailed off as she saw him properly for the first time.

As their eyes met her breath jammed in her throat and her mouth fell open.

Wow.

The man was stunning. Seriously, breathtakingly good-looking.

She knew she was staring but she couldn't help it. What woman wouldn't stare when confronted by a man like this one?

His hair was too long and there was at least two days' growth of stubble around his jaw, but never in her life had she been faced with a vision of such raw, untamed masculinity. Her eyes feasted slowly on the lean perfection of his face, the bold, dark eyebrows and firm, unsmiling mouth.

A long silence stretched between them and finally he spoke. 'What's the matter?' His tone was rough. 'Now that you've seen me properly, are you finally thinking that you might have been foolish to climb into my car?'

'No.' She shook herself and smiled at him, incurably honest. 'Actually, I was thinking that when women kiss you, they probably keep their eyes open.'

He seemed to have lost his powers of speech and she tilted her head to one side and looked at him curiously.

'What's the matter? I'm just saying that you're so good-looking it would be a terrible waste to close your eyes.' She gave an impish smile and he shot her a look of pure, undiluted disbelief.

'Do you always say exactly what's in your head without any thought for the consequences?'

'Always,' she confessed. 'I can't stand people who say one thing and mean another. And don't tell me no one's ever told you you're good-looking before. You must have heard it a million times.'

He studied her, not a flicker of expression on his hand-some face. 'Not usually in these circumstances.'

'You're shocked, aren't you? But I don't see why. You must know you're good-looking.' She shrugged. 'It's no big deal. Just a statement of fact. Like saying it's raining.'

'Raining…' He gave her an odd look. 'Right.'

'Well, at the end of the day looks aren't important, are they?' she said simply. 'Being with a person is about loving them for what's inside, not for what's outside.'

His dark eyes gleamed strangely in the darkness. 'Absolutely.'

Ellie wriggled down in the seat and placed her feet on the heater to warm them. 'I mean, someone can be rich and good-looking but what use is that if they're no fun to be with?'

'What use indeed?' His eyes narrowed slightly as he watched her antics from his side of the car. 'Are you sure you're quite comfortable?'

'Perfectly, thank you.' She beamed at him happily, ignoring the sarcasm in his tone. 'I'm still pretty cold but this is a great car. Your heater is very efficient.'

'I'm glad you approve.' His tone was dry. 'And now are you going to tell me what you were doing, risking your neck driving around on a night like this?'

Ellie gasped and slapped her hand over her mouth. For a brief few moments she'd totally forgotten about Lindsay. 'Oh, heavens. Lindsay! You have to drive me to the top of the lane, quickly. We can't spend any more time chatting.'

'*We?*'

'All right.' She blushed prettily. 'So I'm the one that did the chatting, but now can we make a move? Please! We've wasted so much time already. It's an emergency.'

He didn't shift in his seat. 'What sort of an emergency? Don't tell me—another sheep?'

'Not a sheep. It's my cousin. She thinks she's in labour,' Ellie explained quickly, and he lifted a dark brow.

'She *thinks* she's in labour?'

Ellie shrugged helplessly. 'Well, it's her first baby and it's four weeks early so we're hoping she's wrong.'

'And you're a midwife?'

'Sadly, no. I'm an A and E nurse.' She swallowed and secured the blanket more firmly around her shoulders. 'The midwife is trapped on the other side of the valley—the wrong side of the floods. I don't think she's had much experience of driving through fords.'

'Clearly a sensible woman,' he observed, and Ellie pulled a face.

'A bit pathetic, actually, but there we are. She's coming the long way round, which is going to take her ages. Fortunately she didn't sound that worried on the phone. It's Lindsay's first baby, and she doesn't think it will come for a while yet, but I'm not so sure…' She broke off and he lifted an eyebrow.

'And why is that?'

'Because I've got one of my feelings.' She wrinkled her nose anxiously. 'Which is a problem because I didn't even get a chance to consult my textbook before I came out.'

'And are your—er—*feelings* usually reliable?'

'Always,' Ellie said firmly, cuddling the blanket more tightly around her. Her teeth were starting to chatter and she'd never felt so cold in her life. 'And on top of that her husband is away so, you see, I absolutely have to get to her.'

'Right.' His long fingers tapped the steering-wheel. 'But it wouldn't exactly have improved the situation if you'd drowned yourself and all the rescue services had been forced to come out to extricate you from the river.'

'They wouldn't have been able to. There's been a pile-up on the motorway, which is why they weren't any use to Lindsay.' She twisted in her seat and looked at him with concern. 'Are you hungry?'

'Hungry?' He was clearly taken aback by the question. 'What on earth makes you ask that?'

'Because you're very cross,' Ellie pointed out gently, her tone sympathetic. 'You needn't worry. I get cross when I'm hungry, too. You should eat something straight away to get your blood sugar up.'

There was a long pause and when he spoke his voice wasn't quite steady. 'I'm not hungry.'

'Tired, then?'

'Not tired.' He looked at her and shook his head slowly,

exasperation glittering in his dark eyes. 'I've just never met anyone quite like you before.'

'Well, I haven't met anyone like you before either,' Ellie confessed, frowning slightly as she looked at him. 'You may be gorgeous to look at but you're very tense and you don't show your feelings. It's impossible to know what you're thinking by looking at you, which is always a bit worrying in a person. Now, do you think you could just stop lecturing me and give me a lift to the top of the road? While we're sitting here, getting to know each other, she could be in the final stages of labour.'

She could have been mistaken but she thought she detected a glimmer of laughter in his eyes as he flicked off the internal light. 'Come on, then, I'll take you. If I don't, there's no knowing what you'll get up to. You need a bodyguard.'

He released the handbrake and drove up the road, handling the car skilfully as he negotiated the fierce storm and the lethal driving conditions.

'Directions?'

'Further up on the right.' She paused, her teeth chattering, looking for landmarks. 'Stop here!'

The man pulled up and squinted down the dark track. 'I don't see anything.'

'Well, the farmhouse is in a dip.' Ellie released the blanket and he frowned at her.

'What are you doing now?'

'I'll walk from here.'

'Like hell you will.' He muttered something under his breath and swung the vehicle into the lane.

She gasped and grabbed the seat to steady herself as it jolted viciously into the first pothole. 'You can't drive down here. You'll lose your suspension.'

'This is a four-wheel-drive,' he reminded her, his expression grim as he adjusted the headlights, his eyes fixed on the track. 'Just hang on.'

In no position to argue, she did just that, bracing herself as the vehicle lurched from the left to the right.

Finally he reached the end of the lane and they could see that every light in Lindsay's farmhouse was blazing.

He pulled to a halt and unlocked the doors.

In an impulsive gesture, she leaned across, briefly kissed his rough cheek and then shrugged the blanket off her shoulders and grabbed her sodden clothes.

'Thank you, thank you, thank you. You saved my life. Now, go and get yourself something to eat.' She grimaced as she slid her feet into her soaking wet boots and, without giving him a chance to speak, slid out of the car and sprinted to the front door, knowing that it would be open. It was always open. Lindsay refused to lock it.

'Linny?' She paused in the hallway and shouted for her cousin. 'Lin? It's me. Where are you?'

She heard a muffled sob and took the stairs two at a time. 'Lindsay?'

Throwing open doors, she charged around the upstairs of the farmhouse until she finally found her cousin crouching in a ball in the bathroom, her face streaked with tears.

'Oh, Lin…' Ellie dropped to her knees and scooped her cousin into her arms. 'It's OK. I'm here now. Everything's going to be fine.'

'I thought no one was ever going to get here—' Lindsay broke off with a gasp of pain and clutched at Ellie's hand. 'Paul's away and it's going to take him hours to get home, the midwife is stranded, I thought I was going to be on my own…'

Ellie hugged her tightly. 'You're not on your own. And you should have known I'd get here.'

Lindsay gave a sob. 'If the midwife couldn't manage it, how come you could?'

'I had a stroke of luck,' Ellie said evasively, not wanting to mention the ford. 'How are you feeling?'

'Scared. It's not meant to come this early, and I'm not meant to be at home. Oh, Ellie, what's going to happen?'

'You're going to have a baby, and it's going to be fine.'

'Ugh!' Lindsay shrank away from her. 'You're soaked!'

'Well, in case you hadn't noticed, there's a storm raging outside,' Ellie reminded her. 'It's raining.'

Lindsay gave a soft gasp of pain and rubbed her bump gently. 'This is the Lake District. It always rains. It has to or we wouldn't have lakes. You'd better help yourself to some dry clothes.'

'In a minute.' Ellie looked at her closely. 'Are you OK?'

'Honestly?' Lindsay bit her lip and shook her head. 'No. I'm really panicking. I know it's all going to go wrong.'

'Why should it go wrong?'

A deep male voice came from behind them and Ellie turned in surprise and shock. For a brief moment she'd forgotten about the man in the car. When she'd left him at a run she'd assumed that he'd be driving back down the lane and out of her life. Instead, he was leaning against the doorway of the bathroom, surveying them both through slightly narrowed eyes.

Lindsay glanced at him and then back at Ellie, her expression bemused. 'I— Who are you?'

'A doctor. In the circumstances, I thought you might be glad of some help.'

Ellie gaped at him. *He was a doctor?* 'You don't look like a doctor.'

'You shouldn't be influenced by appearances.' His gaze mocked her as he reminded her of their earlier conversation and she gave a weak smile.

'*Touché.*'

Lindsay was staring at him. 'You're an obstetrician?'

'No.' His tone was clipped and businesslike. 'But I have

delivered plenty of babies in the course of my career. Your cousin mentioned that she isn't a midwife so I thought I'd better check whether you needed help before I left.'

Ellie felt her body flood with relief. She'd been secretly terrified that she'd end up delivering the baby on her own. But he was a doctor.

He'd saved her life twice in one night.

'We need help,' she said firmly, 'most definitely, don't we, Linny?'

Lindsey looked apprehensive. 'But we don't know him, El.'

'I do. He's already rescued me once tonight already and it's only nine o'clock. Trust me, he's a hero. Cool, calm and totally in control. The perfect person to have around in a crisis. A bit tense, maybe...' Ellie's green eyes twinkled with laughter as she glanced at the stranger '...but he can't help that. I'll make him a bacon sandwich if I get a minute. I'm sure his blood sugar is low.'

'My blood sugar is fine. And I'm beginning to think I should have left you stranded by the side of the road.' He looked at her with exasperation and then his gaze flickered to Lindsey. 'Is she always like this?'

'Worse usually,' Lindsey informed him, a weak smile touching her lips despite her own predicament. 'She's totally irrepressible. Says what she thinks and always laughs at the wrong time.'

Ellie looked indignant. 'I don't see that there's ever a wrong time to laugh.'

Lindsay was staring at the doctor. 'What did you mean when you said you should have left her at the side of the road? Why was she at the side of the road?'

Ellie reached for a towel and started rubbing her hair. 'My car broke down.'

Lindsay's eyes widened. 'Why?'

'Who knows?' Ellie ignored the man's ironic glance. 'Anyway, this man saved me. And his name is—is...'

She broke off and stared at him blankly, suddenly aware that she hadn't even asked his name.

'Maybe you should have asked me that before you climbed into my car and stripped off,' he suggested softly, and Lindsay's expression was comical, her voice little more than a squeak.

'What does he mean, you *stripped off*?'

'I was soaking wet,' Ellie explained quickly, glaring at the man crossly. What was she supposed to have done? Stayed in her sodden clothes?

He watched her for a long moment and a ghost of a smile played around his mouth.

'I'm Ben MacAllister,' he said finally, turning his attention back to Lindsay. 'I can assure you that I've delivered babies on several occasions in conditions far more challenging than this.'

Ellie looked at her cousin. 'There we are. Fate brought him to your doorway.'

Lindsay put a hand on hers and took a deep breath, clearly battling with a contraction. After about a minute she spoke again. 'I don't know. I...' She dropped her voice, clearly embarrassed. 'We don't know him, Ellie. And we don't really need him. You could do it if you had to.'

Oh, no, she couldn't!

Ellie patted Lindsay's hand and shot Ben a pleading glance. No way did she want him leaving!

'Lindsay, I'm an A and E nurse, not a midwife,' she pointed out hastily. 'I'll be here to help Ben and give you moral support, but I can't take responsibility. You know I can't. It wouldn't be right. And I've known him long enough to know we can trust him. And, anyway, I've got one of my feelings.'

Lindsay groaned. 'Good or bad?'

'Good,' Ellie said in a definite tone. She had to convince Lindsay. They needed a doctor.

Her eyes slid to his broad frame but he was still watching Lindsay, his eyes flicking down to his watch as she was racked by another contraction.

'Only three minutes since the last one,' he said softly. 'I'd say this baby is in rather a hurry.'

'Oh, God, I didn't want this to happen. I didn't want to have it at home.' Lindsay gave a whimper of panic and Ben crouched down so that he was at her level.

'Home is a great place to have a baby, Lindsay. Where I've been working, home is where everyone has their babies. I realise that you don't know me, and you're right to be cautious...' the look he shot Ellie was meaningful, 'but in this case I promise you can trust me.'

Lindsay stared at him dubiously. 'It's just that, well, you don't look like a doctor.'

That was true enough, Ellie reflected. He looked like a film star.

The corner of his mouth moved slightly. 'Because I need a shave? Do you want me to call someone who can vouch for me? Or you can give me razor and I'll shave here in your bathroom if it will make you feel better.'

There was humour in his tone and something else—a calm confidence that seemed to reassure Lindsay. 'No—there's no need to do that, and I'm sorry if I sound rude but I'm just panicking.' She winced and shifted her position slightly. 'You see, the baby is breech and they think I'll need a section. I'm nobody's idea of a good candidate for a home birth.'

Ben was suddenly still, although his expression didn't change.

'In that case I need to examine you and see if we've time to get you to hospital.'

Not by a flicker of an eyelid did he betray his concern, but Ellie knew he must have felt it. Even with her limited obstetric experience, she knew that breech births should take place in hospital.

Lindsay was looking at him with frightened eyes. 'And what if there isn't time? What happens then?'

'Then I deliver a breech here.' He sounded so relaxed and confident that even Lindsay started to look less traumatised.

'And have you done that before?'

'Of course.'

Ellie looked at him curiously, wondering if he was bluffing. Had he really delivered a breech?

Lindsay still looked worried. 'Everyone told me that breech babies should be born in hospital. What if it all goes wrong—?'

'It won't go wrong.' Ben rose to his feet with athletic grace, totally in control and sensationally attractive. 'It seems to me that three of us and a baby cramped together in this small bathroom is pushing the realms of comfort. Let's move into your bedroom, shall we? Then I can take a look at you. If there's time to get you to hospital, I promise that I'll get you there.'

Lindsay looked at him and then nodded, and Ellie breathed a sigh of relief.

CHAPTER TWO

WITH considerable help from Ben, Lindsay struggled through to the bedroom and settled down on the bed with a groan.

'Don't get too comfortable,' Ben said immediately, pulling off his jacket and tossing it to one side. 'I'm just going to nip down to my car for my bag and then I'm going to examine you.'

Ellie glanced sideways at her cousin, knowing what a private person she was and wondering how she'd react to the prospect of being examined by Ben, but Lindsay was breathing steadily, clearly thinking of nothing but her baby.

Ben strode out of the room and was back only minutes later, a large bag in his hand.

Lindsay lifted her eyebrows and gave a weak smile. 'You must have been a Scout. Are you always this prepared?'

'Since I started working in remote parts of the world.' Ben gave a glimmer of a smile as he pushed up his sleeves and made for the bathroom. 'Experience has taught me that it's wise to always carry at least a basic supply of equipment with me.'

'You don't need to use that bathroom,' Lindsay called after him. 'I was only in there because I was cleaning it. There's an *en suite* over there…'

She gestured with her head and Ben followed her instructions, grunting with satisfaction as he found the large bathroom.

Ellie was staring at her cousin in disbelief. 'Why were

you cleaning the bathroom? You're in labour, for goodness' sake.'

Lindsay shrugged sheepishly. 'Nesting, I suppose. I decided it needed doing.'

'You're mad,' Ellie stated with conviction, glancing up as Ben called over his shoulder from the bathroom.

'Can you run me through your obstetric history while I wash my hands? This is your first pregnancy—correct?' He turned on the hot tap and reached for the soap.

Lindsay answered his questions as thoroughly as she could before breaking off and whimpering as another pain hit her. 'Oh, Ellie…'

'Breathe with her,' Ben instructed over his shoulder as he lathered his hands and forearms with soap, 'and then get me some clean towels.'

He certainly wasn't given to small talk, Ellie mused as she held Lindsay's hand and reminded her how to breathe.

Lindsay followed her cousin's cue and breathed out slowly, perspiration glistening on her forehead.

'I'm OK now. Thanks. You know where the towels are.'

Quickly Ellie fetched the towels and piled them on the chair.

Ben helped himself and then sat down on the edge of the bed. 'OK, this is what we're going to do. First of all Ellie is going to have a hot shower and change out of those wet things. While she's doing that, I'm going to take a look at you so that we know what we're dealing with.'

Ellie suddenly realised that seeing Lindsay had distracted her from the fact that she was freezing cold.

Without further argument, she reached into her cousin's wardrobe and dragged out a pair of jeans and a soft jumper and made for the shower.

Five minutes later her skin was glowing pink and warm from the hot water and the shivering had stopped. She dried her hair roughly with the damp towel and then walked quickly back into the bedroom, startled to see Lindsay smiling. What on earth had made her smile? Not Ben surely?

He glanced at her and his own smile faded, his dark gaze suddenly hard. 'Get back in that bathroom and dry your hair properly.'

Obviously the smile was reserved for Lindsay.

Rolling her eyes, she returned to the bathroom, picked up the hair-dryer and waved it absently in the direction of her hair until it fell in soft, dark waves around her shoulders.

Lindsay looked at her critically as she walked back into the room. 'You'd better help yourself to a belt or you're going to lose those jeans.'

Ellie glanced down at herself, a rueful expression on her face. It was true that the jeans were loose, but they'd do.

'Look at her,' Lindsay murmured to Ben as she rubbed a hand over her stomach. 'She puts on my pre-pregnancy jeans and they're too loose. I hate her. She's got legs up to her armpits and boobs to die for, and the worse thing is she never notices.'

'It's just a body, Lindsay,' Ellie mumbled. 'Everyone's got one.'

Lindsay opened her mouth to say something else and then groaned as another contraction hit her. Ellie was by her side in an instant, holding her cousin's hand and helping her breathe slowly.

'I can feel something! It's coming, I know it is. Oh, Ellie do something!' Lindsay clutched her hand tightly and Ellie looked helplessly at Ben.

'Get me some more light,' he ordered, tugging on a pair of gloves and preparing to examine Lindsay again. 'Lindsay, I'm going to take a look now and see what's going on.'

Ellie grabbed a bedside lamp and removed the shade,

exposing the bulb, while Lindsay looked on anxiously, her eyes brimming with tears.

'Well?'

Ben's face gave nothing away and when he spoke his tone was casual. 'Well, you're right when you say it's coming. I can see a little bottom.'

'Little? If it's a *little* bottom it can't be yours, Linny,' Ellie joked, trying to lighten the atmosphere in the room.

Lindsay gave a weak smile, but there was no disguising her panic. 'So it's too late to go to hospital?'

'Before the birth, yes,' Ben said calmly. 'After you've had the baby we'll get you there. I want you to stand up, Lindsay, and hang onto Ellie. Arms around her neck, feet wide apart… That's it—great.'

'It's going to fall on the floor,' Lindsay muttered, and Ben shook his head.

'It's not going to fall anywhere. Trust me, Lindsay. Just hang onto Ellie and do as I say.'

Ellie winced as Lindsay's fingers dug into her shoulders.

'That's good, Lindsay. Well done.' Ben's voice was deep and reassuring, his movements steady and confident as he worked. 'That's the bottom and the legs delivered.'

Lindsay gave a sob. 'Is its head stuck?'

'It's not stuck. But we don't rush this bit,' Ben explained. 'The head has to be delivered slowly. Just breathe and be patient.'

Two minutes later Lindsay dug her nails into Ellie's shoulders again and there was a sudden wailing, just as they heard footsteps on the stairs.

'Congratulations,' Ben said softly. 'You have a little girl.'

'The door was open so I let myself in. I hope you don't mind.' The midwife bustled into the room and broke off in astonishment at the sight of the bawling baby in Lindsay's arms. 'So you *were* in labour.'

Ellie caught Ben's eye and looked away again quickly.

'It would appear that way,' he drawled.

The midwife was staring at him with shock and blatant disapproval. 'You delivered the baby?'

Ben didn't spare her a glance, instead focusing all his attention on Lindsay.

'He's a doctor,' Lindsay said weakly, and the midwife seemed flustered.

'Oh. Well, naturally I didn't think… I mean, he doesn't look…'

Satisfied that all was still well with Lindsay, Ben lifted his dark head, his handsome face blank of expression. 'As you're here, you can take over and deliver the placenta. I didn't have any Syntometrine so at the moment she's having a physiological third stage.'

'What on earth is that?' Lindsay looked worried and the midwife was quick to explain, dragging her gaze away from Ben with visible effort.

'It means that we haven't given you an injection to make your uterus contract, but its nothing to worry about. It's quite capable of doing it by itself. It will be no problem at all for a young, healthy thing like you.'

The midwife hurried to the bathroom and scrubbed her hands, talking over her shoulder as she did so. 'I came as quickly as I could but the roads are terrible. There's an awful storm outside.'

Ellie caught Ben's eye again and this time failed to stifle a giggle. The midwife had a real talent for stating the obvious. She was beginning to think that Lindsay had had a lucky escape.

Lindsay obviously thought so too because she struggled to sit up, panic in her eyes as she looked at Ben.

'Please, don't leave me.' She glanced furtively towards the bathroom. 'I—I really want you to be here. I trust you.'

Ben was still for a moment. 'I'm not leaving you,' he

said, his voice rough and yet gentle at the same time. 'I'm going to warm the car up so that I can drive you both to hospital once the midwife has delivered the placenta.'

At that moment the midwife bustled out of the bathroom and overheard the last comment.

'Oh, she won't be going anywhere for a while. The roads—'

'I'll worry about the roads,' Ben said tersely. 'You worry about the placenta.'

The midwife looked taken aback. 'Oh— Well, yes…'

Ben strode out of the room and Ellie flung open the wardrobes and found some warm clothes for Lindsay.

'Where have you stashed all the baby things, Linny?'

'In the chest of drawers in the box room.' Lindsay gave a moan. 'Ellie, will you hold her for a minute? Just until we get this bit over with?'

Ellie took the baby immediately, staring in awe at its delicate features. 'Oh, you are so beautiful,' she cooed. 'No way can you be Lindsay's…'

Lindsay gave a weak laugh and the midwife gave a grunt of satisfaction as she finally delivered the placenta.

'There we are, pet. All done.' She checked it carefully and dropped it into a kidney dish. 'Now then, let's get that baby on the breast to help your uterus contract.'

She helped Lindsay sit up and Ellie handed the baby back, still misty-eyed from the experience.

The baby was gorgeous.

'Right.' She cleared her throat and pulled herself together. 'Baby clothes.'

Ben appeared in the doorway, his handsome features unsmiling. 'How is she doing?'

'All finished,' the midwife said briskly. 'Just having a little feed.'

Ellie smiled. 'Come and see her, Ben—she's beautiful!'

Was it her imagination or did his entire body tense?

'I need to make a phone call,' he said curtly. 'Dress both of them warmly and I'll meet you downstairs in five minutes.'

Ellie watched as he strode out of the room, wondering what on earth was wrong. Because something *was* wrong, she was sure of that.

She had one of her feelings...

Ben had saved the baby's life. He'd been warm and kind to Lindsay, but now he was remote and untouchable again. *Why?*

The midwife went downstairs to fetch something from her car and Ellie and Lindsay were finally left alone.

Lindsay turned to her with an excited smile. 'Ellie, he's gorgeous!'

'He?' Bemused, Ellie stared at the baby and then at her cousin. 'It's a girl!'

'I'm not talking about the baby!' Lindsay rolled her eyes. 'I'm talking about *Ben*. Superman, or rather Superdoctor. Where on earth did you find him?'

Ellie hesitated. 'I told you. My car broke down.'

'And?' Lindsay looked at her. 'When my car breaks down I get the AA. I don't get anyone like Ben.'

Ellie rubbed the toe of her shoe on the carpet. 'I flagged him down.'

'You thumbed a lift?' Lindsay's voice rose. 'Ellie, you shouldn't take such risks! It's dark, for goodness' sake!'

'You sound exactly like him.' Ellie suppressed a yawn. 'He's done nothing but lecture me since I climbed into his car.'

'And he's right!' Lindsay looked troubled. 'There are some real perverts in the world, El.'

Ellie sighed. 'You've been reading too many newspapers. Does he look like a pervert to you?'

'No.' Lindsay gave a sheepish grin. 'He's gorgeous. One hundred per cent virile male. Rough and wicked-looking.

The sexiest man I've ever seen—apart from Paul, of course,' she added hurriedly. 'So what are you going to do about it?'

'Do? What do you mean, what am I going to do about it?' Ellie stared at her and laughed. 'What do you expect me to do?'

'I don't know—but *something*.' Lindsay's eyes were shining with excitement. 'You can't let a man like that go to waste. Why not tell him you think he's gorgeous and see what happens?'

'I've done that already,' Ellie confessed with a faint smile. 'He was shocked.'

Lindsay gasped. 'You *told* him he was gorgeous?'

'Well, he is.' Ellie shrugged dismissively. 'It's just the truth.'

'Yes, but most people don't often tell the truth,' Lindsay pointed out, laughing until she clutched her sides with a groan. 'Don't make me laugh—I'm sore all over.'

'I'm not trying to make you laugh and frankly I don't see what's so funny. Now he obviously thinks I'm a tart as well as reckless,' Ellie said gloomily, and Lindsey burst into further noisy laughter.

'A tart? You? Oh, that's rich. You've never even had a proper boyfriend.'

'Will you keep your voice down?' Ellie glared at her and Lindsay covered her mouth with her hand to stifle her laughter.

'Sorry. It's just that you've always said that you've never met anyone worth the effort.' The laughter turned to speculation. 'He might be worth the effort, Ellie.'

Ellie looked disapproving. 'Linny, I've only just met the man! And, anyway, he makes me nervous.'

'Does he now?' Lindsay's eyes were searching. 'Well, that might be a good sign. Why does he make you nervous?'

'I don't know…' Ellie gave a small shrug and stared at her fingers. 'He's very…controlled. And self-contained. And disapproving. I suppose he's just different from the men I'm used to mixing with.'

'That's because you mix with a crowd of boys, not men,' Lindsay said softly, 'and there's nothing boyish about Ben MacAllister. He's a cool-headed, self-possessed, incredibly sexy man.'

'Lindsay, you've just had a baby,' Ellie reminded her. 'You shouldn't be thinking about sex.'

'I'm not thinking about sex for me,' Lindsay defended herself. 'I'm thinking about sex for *you*.' She gazed down at the baby and then looked at Ellie with a contemplative look on her face. 'I just want you to meet someone special. You're so pretty. I have no idea how you've kept men at bay for so long.'

Ellie shrugged and blushed slightly. 'You know why. I just haven't ever met anyone that I've wanted to—that's seemed…' She broke off and gave a shrug. 'That's seemed like the right man to—to—you know.'

'Well, you couldn't do better than Ben MacAllister.' Lindsay gave her a dreamy look. 'You only have to look at him to see that he would definitely know what to do with a woman in bed.'

'Lindsay, those hormones are going to your head!' Ellie started to laugh, her expression shocked and exasperated. 'I've told you, I've only just met him.'

She hadn't even thought of Ben MacAllister in those terms. And she didn't intend to.

It was too unsettling.

She helped dress the baby and Lindsay in warm clothes, and then sprinted down the stairs to find Ben.

He was in the kitchen, talking quietly into his phone. As she walked into the room, his gaze flickered to hers and he quickly finished his conversation and looked at her questioningly.

'Is she ready?'

For a moment Ellie stood rooted to the spot, remembering what Lindsay had said about him knowing what to do with a woman in bed. Her eyes rested on his broad shoulders and then drifted down to the long, powerful legs and she blushed slightly.

Oh, for heaven's sake!

'Ellie?' His voice was sharp and she jumped slightly, hoping that he couldn't read her mind.

Blow Lindsay and her fantasies! She couldn't relate properly to the man any more.

'Er, she's fine, considering.' She couldn't keep the admiration out of her eyes. 'You were amazing. I know how difficult that delivery was, but you made it look like a picnic.'

'We were lucky,' he said grimly, and she shook her head.

'No.' Her voice was soft. 'You were skilled. Don't think I can't see that, and don't think I'm not grateful because I am. Very.'

His dark eyes rested on hers for a long moment and a shiver ran through her.

He really was astonishingly attractive.

She pulled herself together. 'I've been thinking about what you were saying about taking her to hospital. Maybe the midwife is right. Maybe we should wait until the storm dies down. They both seem OK for the moment and those potholes—'

'Scared, Ellie?' He lifted one dark eyebrow a fraction, his tone faintly mocking. 'This from the girl who drove through a flood, flagged down a stranger and ripped off most of her clothes in my car? Are you trying to convince me that you've finally developed a sense of danger?'

'I'm not scared!' She glared at him and then gave a worried sigh. 'Well, not for myself. For Lindsay and the baby. I just think maybe now the baby has been safely delivered, maybe we should wait—'

'We're not waiting.' Ben thrust the phone into the pocket of his jeans and strode past her but she caught his arm.

'Less than an hour ago you were telling me off for driving in that storm.'

His gaze was steady. 'But this time I'll be driving.'

She was outraged. 'You're a total chauvinist!'

'Ellie, engage your brain.' His voice was weary. 'I have a car which is designed to operate in this weather. Your cousin has just had a difficult delivery. The longer we leave it, the worse the roads will get. I think everything is fine, but I'm not an obstetrician or a paediatrician and I'm not taking any chances. She's going to hospital right now.'

Without waiting for a response from her, he strode out of the room and up the stairs to Lindsay, leaving Ellie staring after him.

He was right, of course. It was important to get Lindsay to the hospital. She hurried back out to the hall and glanced up the stairs. Ben tossed her his car keys.

'Get some blankets and put them on the back seat. Strap her baby seat into the car and I'll bring them out in a minute. The heating is already on full.'

Without waiting to argue, Ellie did as he instructed, sprinting back to the bedroom and dragging blankets out of the cupboard.

At the top of the stairs she slithered past Ben who was supporting Lindsay and carrying the baby.

She opened the front door and gasped at the strength of the wind.

The temperature had dropped and the freezing rain had

turned to snow, the huge white flakes reducing visibility even further.

It was not a good night to be out in a car.

Pushing the thought aside, she made a dash for it, opened the back door and threw the blankets inside the car. She had no doubt that Ben was preparing for all eventualities but she didn't even want to consider the possibility that they might be trapped in there.

Fastening her seat belt with frozen fingers, she glanced up to see Ben in the doorway with the baby in his arms. It was so well wrapped up it was barely visible.

Seconds later Lindsay was in the car and the baby was safely strapped in next to her.

'I'm scared she'll get cold,' Lindsay breathed, and Ben slammed the car door shut and checked the heating.

'Keep those blankets on her and she'll be fine. She's had a feed so that should help. I'll drive as carefully as I can but this might be a rough ride,' he warned them as he climbed into the driver's seat and started the engine.

The midwife waved them off and they made it back down the farm track with no problem and turned onto the lane that ran near Lindsay's farm.

Ellie saw Ben's fingers tighten on the steering-wheel and knew from the tension in his shoulders that the roads were bad, the snow making the driving conditions slushy and dangerous.

'The quickest way to the hospital is back through the ford,' she said quietly, and she saw him nod briefly.

How long had they been at Lindsay's?

How much rain had fallen in that time?

As he approached the water Ellie closed her eyes and held onto Lindsay's hands, but she needn't have worried. The four-wheel-drive barely hesitated as it plunged happily through the water and up the other side.

Lindsay looked out of the back window and gasped.

'There's your little car.' Suddenly understanding dawned and she stared at Ellie, horrified. 'Oh, my God! You broke down because you drove through the ford, didn't you? That's why you got to me so quickly! Oh, Ellie! Whatever made you take such a risk?'

'I love you,' Ellie mumbled, 'and no one else seemed prepared to try it. Don't worry about the car. I'll sort it out tomorrow.'

'I'm not worried about your car, I'm worried about you!'

'Don't be.' Ellie gave her a cheerful smile. 'I'm not the one who's just had an upside-down baby.'

'She was the right way up,' Lindsay pointed out, and Ellie shook her head.

'No. Medically speaking she was upside down.' She chatted away, distracting Lindsay as Ben negotiated the lethal road conditions. Once they hit the main road things improved slightly and Ben handed her his phone without taking his eyes off the road. The snow was falling silently onto the windscreen, obscuring his vision.

'Call A and E. Ask for Sean Nicholson. Tell him our ETA is five minutes. Ask him if we go to A and E or the labour ward. I spoke to him earlier and he should have fixed something up by now.'

Ellie stared at him, puzzled. Sean was the consultant in charge of the A and E department. How did Ben know him?

She shook herself and punched the number into the phone. Now wasn't the time to worry about things like that or to tell him that she worked in that department and knew Sean very well herself.

She spoke to the receptionist and got through to Sean easily.

It was clear that Ben had already briefed him fully. 'They're expecting her on the labour ward,' he said immediately. 'Get MacAllister to use Entrance 6 and pull the car right up to the door. There's a midwife waiting for her.'

'We'll be five minutes.'

Ellie handed the phone back to Ben, relayed Sean's instructions and gave Lindsay's hand a squeeze.

Lindsey looked at her, her eyes overly bright in the darkness. 'Well, this wasn't exactly what you'd call a textbook delivery.'

'And since when has life gone according to the books? Mine never does,' Ellie pointed out, and Lindsay grinned.

'That's because you read romance novels. Life is never like that.'

Briefly Ellie caught Ben's glance in the rear-view mirror and then he was pulling up outside the entrance of the hospital.

'OK, we're here. Let's get you checked out.'

Without further conversation he undid Lindsay's seat belt, scooped her up in his arms as if she weighed nothing and walked briskly the short distance to the medical team who were waiting with a wheelchair.

Then he returned to collect the baby.

Ellie followed, surprised to see Sean Nicholson hovering. 'Hello, handsome. What's an A and E consultant doing in a place like this?' she quipped, and he gave a lop-sided smile.

'Interfering. Checking that the obs team are doing their job.'

'Well, thanks a lot, Nicholson.' Jed Matthews, the obstetric consultant, glared at him and then smiled at his patient. 'Hello, Lindsay. I hear you've been giving everyone heart failure.'

Lindsay stared at all the doctors in amazement. 'Why am I getting all this attention? The baby's been born!'

'Well, you're our VIP this week.' Jed laughed. 'That

and the fact that, for some unknown reason, we're not busy at the moment. Give me the low-down, Ben.'

'It was a breech delivery but everything seemed fairly straightforward…' Ben raked his dark hair out of his eyes as he ran Jed through the details of the delivery and then turned to Lindsay and gave her a brief smile. 'You were brave. You did well.'

He turned on his heel but Lindsay reached out a hand to stop him leaving.

'Wait!' Her tone was urgent. 'You can't go! Not just like that. I haven't thanked you for everything you've done. Paul is going to want to talk to you. If it hadn't been for you…' She bit her lip, visibly flustered. 'Where can I get hold of you?'

Ben's cool expression softened slightly. 'You don't need to get hold of me,' he said, his tone neutral, 'and no thanks are needed.'

With that he shook off her hand, gave a brief nod and followed Sean Nicholson down the corridor towards the accident and emergency department.

Lindsay gave Ellie a helpless look and Ellie shrugged. What did Lindsay expect her to do? Run after the man? Hardly.

The priority now was Lindsay and the baby. Still anxious about her cousin, she turned to Jed whom she knew from her work in A and E. 'Can I stay with her? At least until Paul gets here?'

Jed nodded. 'Of course. OK, folks, let's move. Let's check the two of them out.'

Some time later a more relaxed Lindsay was cuddling her baby daughter and Ellie was slumped, exhausted, on a chair next to her bed.

'How come I'm so tired when you're the one with a new baby?'

'But you forded streams and climbed mountains to get to me.' Lindsay's expression was grateful. 'I love you, Ellie.'

Ellie grinned. 'I love you, too. And next time you have a baby, do me a favour and move somewhere civilised. Either that or at least have it in the summer and in daylight. What are you going to call her?'

Lindsay stroked the baby's downy head. 'Storm.'

'What?' Ellie couldn't hide her astonishment and Lindsay smiled.

'Don't look like that. I always wanted a name that was slightly different and I think it suits her. She was born in a storm, it's easy to spell and no one else at school will have the same name so she won't have trouble with her coat peg.'

Ellie blinked. 'Storm…Storm…' She tried it out a few times and nodded slowly. 'Actually, I like it. But shouldn't you wait to ask Paul?'

'Wait to ask me what?' Right on cue, Lindsay's husband Paul strode into the room and scooped his wife and daughter into his arms. 'I'm so sorry, Linny.'

'So you should be.'

He closed his eyes and dropped a kiss on her forehead. 'Beat me up. Go on. Do anything you like.'

Lindsay smiled placidly. 'Don't tempt me,'

Still holding his wife, Paul's gaze rested on Ellie. 'You were with her?'

'The whole time,' Ellie said softly, sharing a warm look with her cousin. 'But now I'm going to leave the two of you alone. I'm nipping down to A and E. I suspect they're having a bad night.'

And she owed it to them to help out if she could.

She slipped out of the room, ruefully aware that Lindsay and Paul were so wrapped up in their new baby that they'd barely noticed her leave.

*   *   *

A and E was in chaos.

'Get him into Crash—now!' Nicky, the A and E sister, gestured to the paramedics and looked up in relief when she saw Ellie walking towards them. 'Oh, boy, am I glad to see you. We've been phoning around for extra staff but most people are stranded because of the storm. Is it too much to hope that you're here to help out?'

Ellie smiled. 'I'm all yours. I'll go and get changed, shall I?' She was still in the jeans and jumper that she'd borrowed from Lindsay and Nicky shook her head, bustling her along the corridor.

'No time. Frankly, I don't care if you're wearing a bikini as long as you're here. If I get a minute I'll send someone to find you a white coat. In the meantime, can you go to Resus? The Mountain Rescue Ream are bringing in a ripe case of hypothermia. A woman reported missing two days ago.'

Ellie nodded. 'ETA?'

'Five minutes. You should have time to get the room ready and grab yourself a doctor if you can find one. They're a rare commodity at the moment. There's been a pile-up on the motorway, but I suppose you know about that.'

She did indeed.

Thinking of Lindsay's lucky escape, Ellie walked briskly to the large Resuscitation room, pushed open the doors and started to prepare the necessary equipment.

Being the only hospital in the area, they were used to dealing with cases brought in from the mountains, including people suffering from hypothermia.

Once she was satisfied that she'd prepared the room as best she could, she left Resus and went in search of a doctor.

She found Sean Nicholson in his office on the telephone, arguing with a junior doctor about beds.

'I can't keep her overnight in my department.' Sean caught sight of Ellie and rolled his eyes before turning his attention back to the phone. 'Yes, I understand you're full, so transfer someone or phone your consultant.' His mouth tightened as he listened to the response. 'Well, get him out of bed!'

He replaced the phone, not bothering to hide his irritation. 'Why do other consultants get to sleep at night while I'm here, slaving away?'

'Because you love it,' she reminded him with a smile, and he shook his head ruefully and then looked at her quizzically.

'What are you doing here anyway? I thought you were staying with your cousin?'

'I was, but she's fine and her husband is here now so I'm redundant.' Ellie's smile faded. 'Mountain Rescue just called. A woman has been lost on the fells for two days so at the very least she must be hypothermic. I need a doctor in Resus.'

'A doctor? What's that?' Sean's tone was short and bitter. 'They're an endangered species around here.' His gaze flickered to the sofa in the corner of his office and for the first time Ellie realised that someone else was in the room.

'MacAllister?' Sean's voice was weary. 'I know you've already delivered a baby tonight and you're not officially starting for another two days, but this is right up your street and I'm pushed for staff. I don't suppose you can be persuaded to help out?'

There was a long silence and then Ben MacAllister rose to his feet. 'I thought you were afraid I'd frighten the patients,' he drawled, and Sean shrugged, clearly harassed.

'This one's unconscious so she'll never know you look dark and dangerous. And, anyway, it's the middle of the night. The one thing you can be sure of in this hospital is that no one from the management team will be around after six o'clock in the evening.' He didn't bother to disguise the bitterness in his tone. 'Just promise me you'll shave before you start work officially or the powers that be will think I've employed a savage. This is Ellie, by the way, one of our staff nurses, but I suppose you know that as you delivered her cousin's baby. Ellie, this is Ben. Don't judge by appearances—he's a fantastic doctor.'

'I never judge by appearances.' Ellie was staring at Ben. 'You're working here?'

'Well, what sort of a welcome is that?' Sean was looking at her with astonishment. 'This is Dr MacAllister and he's working as a locum consultant for six months. Knowing how desperate we are for staff, you should be on your knees, kissing his feet.'

Ellie grinned. She was used to Sean's endless banter and it made her laugh. Everyone in A and E was the same. It was the liveliest place she'd ever worked and the teamwork was amazing, mostly because Sean Nicholson was such a great boss.

'I've already kissed him once tonight,' she said lightly, 'and he looked distinctly shocked, so the next time there's any kissing, it's got to come from him. I'll be in Resus when you're ready.'

With that she turned on her heel and left the room, aware that they were both staring after her.

CHAPTER THREE

'SHE kissed you?' Sean grinned at his friend and folded his arms across his chest. 'In that case I'd say you've got some serious explaining to do.'

Ben shook his head and a ghost of a smile touched his firm mouth. 'That girl is unbelievable.' He briefly described the events of the evening leading up to arriving at Lindsay's, and Sean threw back his head and laughed.

'She drove through the ford?' His eyes gleamed with admiration. 'Good old Ellie! That requires some nerve in a car like hers.'

'Nerve?' Ben gave a disapproving frown. 'You're as bad as she is! It's not funny, Sean. She could have been swept away. And she's so damn trusting.' He broke off and Sean looked at him keenly.

'Meaning?'

Ben breathed out heavily and raked his fingers through his dark hair. He had a very clear memory of the way her damp shirt had clung to the contours of her body.

'She thumbed a lift, climbed into the car with me and then treated me as though she'd known me all her life. And, yes, she kissed me goodbye.'

'So?' Sean looked amused rather than shocked. 'That's just Ellie. She's warm, loving and very tactile.'

'She's reckless.'

'She's very young,' Sean pointed out in an indulgent tone and Ben was suddenly very still, his eyes slightly narrowed.

Too young.

'I've never met anyone so oblivious to risk.'

'Well, that's probably not her fault, given who her father was.' Sean's tone was thoughtful and Ben lifted an eyebrow.

'Go on, then,' he prompted softly. 'Who was her father?'

'Phil Harrison.'

Ben stared at him, his attention caught. '*The* Phil Harrison? The climber who died on Everest?'

Sean nodded. 'The very same.'

Something struck a chord in Ben's brain and he frowned at his friend. 'I remember reading something about his daughter. Wasn't she there when he was killed by that avalanche?'

Sean nodded, a grim expression on his face. 'She was at Base Camp, yes. Her father took her everywhere with him. Except to the top, of course. But knowing Ellie, she would have gone there, too, given the chance.'

Ben's expression showed his amazement. Ellie had trekked all the way to Everest Base Camp when she'd only been in her teens? She must be tougher than she looked.

'So what happened to her when he died?'

Sean flicked through some papers on his desk. 'Jack Morgan is her uncle. Married to Phil's sister.' Sean tossed the papers to one side and stood up. 'He owns the Outdoor Pursuits Centre in Little Langdale and he's leader of the Mountain Rescue Team. When Phil was killed Ellie went to live with them. Sometimes she helps out at the centre as a climbing instructor. Most of the time we keep her busy here.'

Ben looked at him curiously. 'And is Ellie a member of the Mountain Rescue Team?'

'Oh, yes.' Sean gave a short laugh, as though it was a silly question. 'She's a chip off the old block. An amazing climber. To be precise, she's a member of SARDA.'

The Search and Rescue Dog Association. Like all mountaineers, Ben was well aware of their role in rescuing climbers from the mountains.

'She doesn't look old enough.'

Sean was amused. 'She's no baby, but I suspect she's not particularly worldly either if that's what you're asking. I don't know much about her love life but I suspect she loves her damn dog more than any person.' He gave his friend with a speculative look. 'You're very interested in her all of a sudden.'

'I am not.' Ben's voice was terse as he answered the question and Sean looked at him quizzically.

'Well, maybe you should be. She's a sweetheart.'

'She's also incredibly young.' *Far too young for him.* He'd made that mistake once before in his life. Ben gave a twisted smile and made for the door. 'Time for me to go and help Nurse Harrison, I think, before you turn into Cupid and shoot me with your bow and arrow.'

'Ben, wait.' Sean's voice stopped Ben as he reached the door, and he turned.

'What now?'

Sean rubbed a hand over the back of his neck and didn't even try to disguise the concern in his eyes.

'Will you be OK?'

It was a question he'd been asking himself since he'd walked through the doors of A and E earlier that day.

Ben's knuckles whitened as he gripped the door handle. 'I don't know,' he admitted finally, 'but there's only one way to find out, isn't there?'

Ellie looked up and smiled as Ben strode into the room. 'Hello, there. I've warned X-Ray that we might need them urgently and I've prepared Resus,' she told him briskly, looking away as she talked. *He was so good-looking she found him distracting.* 'And I've put some woollen blankets to warm and dug out some polythene. Is there anything else I should do?'

She dragged on an apron and gloves in readiness and then suddenly realised that Ben seemed to be frozen to the spot.

Plucking up the courage to look at him, she immediately saw the lines of tension around his firm mouth and the bleak expression in his dark eyes. He seemed to be staring at some point in the middle distance, his mind clearly elsewhere.

She frowned with concern. 'Is something wrong?'

For a long moment he didn't answer, his eyes slowly scanning every inch of the room as if searching for ghosts.

Ellie walked across to him, tilting her head so that she could see his face. 'Ben?'

He didn't respond, his body frozen into stillness by some emotion that she didn't begin to comprehend. It was as if he was totally unaware of her presence. Finally, he turned and looked down at her and she was shocked by the raw pain in his eyes.

'Ben, talk to me—please tell me, what's wrong.' Instinctively she reached out to him, placing a hand on his arm, and strangely her touch seemed to reach him in a way that words hadn't.

He drew in a long breath and moved away from her slowly, reluctantly, as if her touch was a lifeline that he was afraid to throw away.

'Nothing's wrong.' His voice was hoarse and Ellie stared at him helplessly.

How could he deny that something was wrong?

She opened her mouth to question him further but there was something about him—something remote and detached—that prevented her from speaking. His broad shoulders were tense and the pain in his eyes was so acute that it hurt to look at him.

For once at a loss for words, Ellie stared at him in silence and then jumped with shock as the doors to Resus slammed open and several members of the Mountain Rescue Team hurried in with a trolley.

Concerned and confused, Ellie sneaked another look at Ben, wondering whether he would be all right to deal with the patient.

He certainly hadn't been all right a moment ago.

At that moment, Sean appeared in the doorway, his tone casual. 'Everything OK?'

On the surface it was an innocent enough question but his eyes were on Ben as he asked it and Ellie gave him a puzzled frown. It was as if Sean knew that there might be a problem.

What problem?

'Jack, you already know Ben MacAllister.' Sean waved a hand. 'He's back working with us for a while.'

Jack looked up with a friendly smile. 'Good to see you, MacAllister! Haven't seen your ugly mug around for a while.'

'Good to see you, too.'

Ellie looked closely at Ben but there was no sign of the tension that had been so clearly visible earlier. Whatever had bothered him, he was clearly back in control now, his movements smooth and confident as he quickly examined the woman.

'What's the story?'

'She's spent two nights lost in the Langdales. OK, let's move her—on my count.' Jack's smile faded as they transferred the unconscious woman onto the A and E trolley. 'She was eventually spotted by a climber who administered first aid, managed to lower her from the ledge to more solid ground and then called us.'

'Good for him.' Ben glanced at Ellie who was checking the thermometer. 'Core temperature?'

'Thirty degrees.'

Ben stared at her. 'You're sure?'

Ellie checked the device again. 'Thirty degrees,' she said firmly, and Jack whistled.

'That is one cold woman. And hardly surprising, considering the weather we had last night. She's been lying in the snow for goodness knows how long.'

One of the casualty officers walked in and strolled over to Ben.

'I'm Will Thacker.' He introduced himself in smooth tones. 'Sean thought you might need some help. I've read all your papers on high-altitude medicine and I'm looking forward to working with you.'

Ellie concentrated on the patient, trying to hide her distaste. She didn't often take a dislike to a person, but she disliked Will. And he made her feel uneasy. For a start, he didn't look her in the eyes when he talked to her—he talked to her chest.

Ben barely spared him a glance. 'OK, she's got severe hypothermia, folks. Let's move!'

Ellie covered the patient with the warmed woollen blankets and layers of polythene.

'I can't find a pulse.' She moved her fingers slightly but shook her head. 'Nothing.'

'Keep checking,' Ben growled. 'Nobody is ever cold and dead. Only warm and dead.'

Ellie nodded, aware that in extreme hypothermia it was sometimes impossible to find a pulse but that the patient could still be alive. As she felt for a pulse she stared down into the woman's face and frowned slightly.

'Ben, we know her.'

Ben glanced up briefly and then returned to what he was doing. 'What are you talking about?'

'Her name is Joanna Kingston.' Ellie turned to one of the junior nurses, her tone urgent. 'Go to Reception and get her notes, will you, please? She was in two months ago with a suicide attempt. Swallowed paracetamol.'

Ben's mouth tightened. 'Suicide attempt? Well, this time she just might have succeeded. If we're not careful she'll go into VF with a core temperature that low.'

'I've got a pulse!' Ellie looked up, triumphant, and Ben gave a brief nod.

'OK, I want U and Es, FBC, toxicology, clotting screens, blood glucose, amylase, blood cultures and ABG.' He glanced up and his eyes narrowed as he looked at Ellie. 'Why are you smiling?'

'You sound like one of those doctors from the movies,' she told him, fishing out the right blood bottles while the casualty officer searched for a vein. 'Just let me know when you're ready for me to mop your fevered brow and swoon at your feet.'

Ben looked at her for a moment and then a ghost of a smile touched his mouth. 'That won't be necessary. Can you arrange an X-ray and an ECG?'

Ellie was already dialling as he spoke, breaking off to speak quickly to X-Ray, her free hand reaching for the ECG machine. 'It's a good job women are good at multi-tasking,' she muttered as she wheeled the machine over to the patient.

Will cursed under his breath. 'I can't find a vein. I think her circulation has collapsed.'

'Let me...' Ben tightened the tourniquet and took hold of the woman's arm, examining it carefully. Seconds later he stuck out a hand. 'Venflon.'

Ellie handed him one immediately and Ben deftly inserted it under the skin, grunting with satisfaction as blood oozed up the cannula.

'Tape it fast before we lose it,' he said tersely, moving back up to the patient's head. 'Give that oxygen through a humidifier,' he instructed, turning to the casualty officer. 'When you send off those blood gases, remember to tell the lab that she's hypothermic. We'll give IV fluids through a warming device and not too fast.'

With an awed expression on his face, Will set to work, following Ben's instructions to the letter, asking questions all the time. 'What happens if we give it too fast? I haven't dealt with a case of hypothermia before.'

Ben's glance rested on Ellie who'd returned to the patient's side. 'Maybe Nurse Harrison can answer that?'

'Testing me, Dr MacAllister?' Ellie smiled cheerfully at Ben but the smile faded rapidly as she turned back to Will and noticed that he was staring at her chest again. Blow the man! 'Give her too much fluid and you might precipitate pulmonary oedema.'

Her tone was flat and Ben gave her a searching gaze before leaning over her shoulder as she positioned the ECG leads.

She flicked the machine on and watched closely. 'Ouch. Look at that.'

'I'm looking. Someone bleep the medical reg,' Ben said, his mouth set in a grim line as he scanned the ECG. 'We're aiming for a core temperature rise of one degree an hour. If we do it too fast we risk causing hypotension and another fall in temperature.'

It was another hour before the team had stabilised the woman and transferred her to the intensive care unit.

'Will she make it, do you think?' Ellie tore off her apron and stuffed it into the bin, her face concerned.

Ben shrugged. 'I don't know. Maybe. If she does, they'll need to arrange a referral to the psychiatrist.'

'Poor thing.' Ellie gave a long sigh. 'I wonder what made her feel so desperate she wanted to kill herself. Terribly sad.'

Sean stuck his head round the door. 'When you've finished here, the two of you should go home. It's almost two a.m. and you must be totally knackered after the night you've had. Ellie, what's happening about your car, sweetheart? Are you going home with Jack?'

'He's already left. I didn't think to ask him.' Ellie bit her lip in dismay. She'd forgotten about her car. And she needed to get back to feed Max. 'Don't worry—I'll cadge a lift from someone or get a taxi.'

'I'll give you a lift, Ellie,' Will said immediately, and Ellie felt her heart sink. That was the last thing she wanted, but she didn't want to be rude.

'She's coming with me.' Ben's tone was abrupt and Will glanced from one to the other and gave a careless shrug.

'Fair enough. I'll see you folks tomorrow, then.'

Ellie watched him go and then turned back to Ben, relief showing on her face. 'How did you know I didn't want to go with him?'

'Because everything you think is either written all over your face or comes out of your mouth,' he said dryly, ripping off his sterile gloves and tossing them into the bin. 'I had the distinct impression that Dr Thacker isn't your favourite person.'

'Well, you're right and that's three times tonight you've rescued me,' she said gratefully. 'But you needn't worry about actually giving me a lift. I can make my own way home.'

'Ellie…' His smile was weary. 'Just get in my car. Otherwise, no doubt, you'll cadge a lift from someone undesirable—not that he'd stand a chance with you. You'd talk him to death before he could do you any harm.'

She gave a brief smile and peeped at him cautiously, wondering whether she dared ask him about what had happened earlier.

No.

He clearly hadn't wanted to talk about it, and this certainly wasn't the right place for tackling something that obviously affected him so deeply.

'You really don't have to take me home. Besides—' her eyes twinkled with humour '—I don't accept lifts from strangers.'

'I'd noticed.' There was a hint of laughter in his eyes. 'Get in my car, Ellie.'

'Well, if you're sure...' Suddenly aware that she felt totally exhausted, she looked at Ben gratefully. 'Is it horribly out of your way? Where are you living?'

Sean glanced at them both and started to laugh. 'He's living next door to you. Did Jack forget to mention it?'

Ellie stared at him, too tired to take it in. 'Didn't Jack mention what?'

'When I told Jack I had a new doctor starting, he offered me one of the log cabins for the winter.' Sean grinned. 'It's the one next door to Ellie's. You're going to be neighbours.'

Neighbours.

As he drove carefully along the rain-slicked roads towards the Outdoor Pursuits Centre, Ben glanced sideways at his passenger and gave a disbelieving shake of his head.

She was fast asleep, and had been from the minute she'd climbed into his car, clearly exhausted.

Now her eyes were closed, dark lashes fanning her cheeks, her soft dark hair half obscuring her features. But he could still see the full mouth and her long slim legs tucked under her on the seat. She slept like a child, blissfully content and relaxed. Even in her sleep she looked happy.

He'd never met anyone quite so unrelentingly cheerful and optimistic. Maybe it was just her youth, he reflected. Life hadn't had time to grind her down.

Ben gave a short laugh. *At least she didn't talk in her sleep.*

Noticing a sign for the centre, he turned right onto a bumpy lane and followed the track down to the small lake, blinking in surprise as he saw a cluster of log cabins nestling among the trees. It was a wonderful setting.

He pulled up outside one of the cabins and checked the number. Sixteen. That was hers. Which meant his must be next door.

He opened the car door, expecting her to wake up, but she didn't stir and he touched her shoulder gently.

'Ellie?' He gave her a gentle shake but her eyes remained closed. Ben gritted his teeth. What was he supposed to do? Carry her into her cabin? There didn't seem to be any other answer.

Feeling as though he were committing a crime, he reached for her bag and found her keys and then walked round to the passenger side.

Releasing her seat belt, he scooped her into his arms, still expecting her to wake up. Instead, she nestled into his chest, her soft hair tickling his chin as she snuggled closer.

He walked across to the door of the cabin, painfully aware of the subtle scent that clung to her. It was a mixture of roses and summer and soft, warm woman, and it had a disturbing effect on him.

What was the matter with him?

So much for telling Sean that he didn't feel anything any more.

It must be the strain of a long and difficult day that was making him react like this.

When he'd walked into Resus tonight for the first time in two years, he'd almost lost it. Two years had suddenly become two seconds and for a moment he'd been trapped by the memories—the smell, the noise and the utter helplessness. He'd been unable to move, unable to function as a doctor.

But then Ellie had touched him.

It was as if her warmth had melted the chill inside him

and brought him back from the edge of hell to a place that was bearable.

It was because of her that he'd been able to cope.

Which didn't bode well for the rest of his stint in A and E, he thought grimly, bringing himself sharply back to the present as he walked to her door. He couldn't exactly ask to have her by his side every time he walked into Resus, could he?

So what was he going to do?

Leave?

Ask Sean if he could work everywhere except Resus?

Hardly. He just needed to work harder at hiding his feelings.

Especially when he was near Ellie.

Despite her endless chatter, she was unusually observant.

As he stood in the doorway to her cabin he stared down into her face, noticing the thick dark lashes and the soft pink mouth.

Her mouth...

Ben remembered her remark about kissing him and his insides tightened.

Damn.

Pulling himself together, he fumbled with the keys, opened the door and found the light switch, blinking in surprise as he looked round her cabin.

It was totally Ellie.

Touches of her warmth and cheerfulness were everywhere. Brightly coloured rugs, cushions and throws over the sofas blended together to make a stylish and cosy home. It was surprisingly large, with picture windows overlooking the lake and a huge log fire that lay stacked with logs ready to be lit.

Where was her bedroom?

He found it through the second door, a pretty room decorated in different tones of green and cream that reminded him of being outdoors.

Careful not to wake her, he laid her gently on the bed, tugged off her boots and covered her with a duvet. That was as far as he was prepared to go.

There was absolutely no way he was undressing her.

It was daylight when Ellie woke and Max, her German shepherd dog, was on the bed, licking her face.

'Oh, yuck. Gross! Get off.' She pushed him away sleepily and then caught sight of the clock. 'Oh, my goodness!'

She sat upright, pushed the duvet down and suddenly realised that she was fully clothed. 'Oh, Max, I must have fallen asleep in his car.'

Swinging her legs out of bed, she stood up and yawned before padding into the huge sitting room and strolling over to the window.

The Outdoor Pursuits Centre consisted of thirty log cabins set in a wood by a lake and a large house which was used for conferences and meetings.

Through the trees she could see the next door cabin and wondered if Ben was awake. If he was, she ought to thank him. She owed him a lot for everything he'd done the day before.

And she wanted to check that he was all right.

She frowned thoughtfully as she remembered what had happened in Resus. It was as if it was the last place in the world he'd wanted to be. But then the patient had arrived and somehow he'd managed to pull himself together.

What had happened in his past to bring that look to his eyes?

She showered and changed quickly and then grabbed a bag and loaded it with the contents of her fridge, before adding a packet of fresh coffee.

'Come on, Max. We're going to cook breakfast. If you

get really lucky, you might be able to have some.' She whistled to the dog, dragged on a fleece and left her cabin without bothering to lock it.

Outside, the rain and the snow had stopped but it was still bitterly cold and her breath clouded the icy air as she walked briskly along the path to the next-door cabin.

She lifted a hand and tapped gently on Ben's door, hoping that she wasn't going to wake him up.

The door opened and she took a step back as she stared at the man in the doorway, thinking for a moment that she was in the wrong cabin.

The long, unruly hair had been cut short and he'd shaved off the stubble.

'Oh…' Flustered by the change in his appearance, she took a step backwards. 'You look different.'

But still staggeringly sexy.

'Did you want something?'

She smiled, refusing to be deflected by his abrupt manner. 'Yes. I wanted to spoil you. I'm cooking you breakfast.'

His frown was less than encouraging. 'Ellie—'

'By my reckoning, you missed dinner last night,' she said quickly. 'Did you eat when you got in?'

'No, but—'

'And have you eaten yet this morning?'

The frown deepened. 'No, but I had—'

'Well, there you are, then!' She beamed at him and rustled the bag temptingly. 'It's the least I can do after everything you did for me yesterday. You rescued me from the storm, delivered my cousin's baby and then saved me from a fate worse than death—a lift from Will! Believe me, I owe you! Just give me ten minutes in your kitchen and you'll feel like a new person. This is Max. I hope you don't mind him joining us.'

Without giving him time to object, she slid past him

into his cabin and made her way to the kitchen area. The layout of all the cabins was the same so she had no problems finding her way around.

In a matter of minutes she was clattering pans and singing to herself while she trimmed fat off bacon and whipped eggs into a creamy froth. Max settled himself by the table, his head on his paws, his eyes never leaving Ellie.

'Coffee or tea?' She glanced at Ben over her shoulder and her insides quaked slightly. He looked dark and forbidding and very, very serious. And he obviously didn't want her in his cabin, making breakfast.

Oh, help. Maybe this was a mistake.

'Coffee,' she said finally in a small voice, trying to ignore the ominous silence. 'It will wake you up.'

'Ellie, why are you doing this?'

She flushed and flipped the bacon over before it could burn, wondering what he'd say if he knew she'd been asking herself the same question. She didn't usually throw herself at men. In fact, she'd never done it in her life before. She just knew that she was desperate to be near him.

'I've told you. You looked after me yesterday so it's my turn to look after you today. I'm sorry I fell asleep in your car. I'm sorry you had to carry me. Did you slip a disc?'

'Hardly.'

Her joke barely raised a smile but his dark eyes skimmed over her figure and she felt herself grow strangely hot.

'You should have woken me up,' she said brightly, and this time the merest hint of a smile touched his firm mouth.

'How? You sleep like the dead.'

'I know.' Ellie gave him an apologetic look. 'I've always been able to sleep anywhere. Nothing disturbs me.' She divided the bacon between two plates and added scrambled eggs, tomatoes and some delicious dark gilled mushrooms. 'There we are. Tuck in.'

She put the plates down on the table and poured the coffee.

'Are you trying to kill me with cholesterol?' He picked up a knife and fork and she watched anxiously, warming her hands around her mug.

'Stop complaining and eat. It will make you feel better.'

He glanced up, his expression unreadable. 'Ellie, I feel fine.'

It was a blatant warning for her to keep her distance but she chose to ignore it. He was obviously far from fine and she desperately wanted to help.

She took a deep breath. 'You look tired.' She tilted her head and scrutinised him closely, taking in the fine lines and shadows around his eyes. 'And stressed. Ben, I saw your face when you walked into Resus last night. What was wrong?'

The atmosphere in the room went from cool to freezing and his jaw tightened. 'Are you always this direct?'

'Always.' She nodded vigorously and then brushed aside a wisp of dark hair that threatened to fall into her coffee. 'I told you that last night. It's always better to speak your mind. It saves a great deal of confusion in the long run.' She hesitated and fiddled with her fork. 'You know, it really might help to talk about it.'

Ben's tone was cool and discouraging. 'Talk about what?'

'Whatever it is that upset you last night. Whatever it is that's making you tense.'

'Ellie...'

His tone was a warning and she dropped her eyes to her plate, wondering what was the matter with her. He was a total stranger. Why did she care so much about him?

Never one to give up easily, she tried again. 'You obviously don't want to talk about whatever it is. But there's no point in you denying that there's something wrong because it's obvious.' She chewed some bacon slowly, her face troubled. 'I know that most men aren't great at showing their feelings, but you might find that it feels better to talk about it and—'

'Ellie!' He interrupted her sharply and she sighed.

'All right, I'll change the subject.' She ate some more bacon and egg. 'So how do you know Sean?'

He paused and then obviously decided that the question was harmless enough. 'We were in medical school together.'

'Wow.' She paused with her fork halfway to her mouth and grinned at the thought. 'I bet the pair of you caused havoc. What was Sean like before he met Ally?'

'Lethal.'

Ellie laughed with delight. 'I thought as much.' She noticed that his plate was empty and smiled with satisfaction. At least he'd eaten something. 'Toast?'

He sat back in his chair and shook his head. 'No, thank you. I couldn't eat another thing.'

'Good.' She picked up his plate and popped it into the dishwasher. 'So how do you know my Uncle Jack?'

He sighed. 'Listen, Ellie…'

She drew breath guiltily. 'Don't tell me, you're not a morning person and I'm talking too much. I do that quite often. I'm sorry,' she said in a conscience-stricken voice. 'Can I stay if I promise not to talk?'

One dark eyebrow lifted. 'Is that possible?'

She considered it carefully. 'All I can say is that I'll try my hardest.'

'I'd hate to subject you to severe strain,' he said dryly. 'Feel free to talk if you feel so inclined.'

'But not about what happened yesterday, I suppose,' she said cautiously, testing the water and then flinching when she saw his face darken ominously, 'All right, whatever is bothering you is a taboo subject from now on.'

'Nothing is bothering me!' His tone was exasperated and he stood up suddenly and paced over to the window. He was silent for a long moment as he stared out over the lake and then he turned and settled himself on one of the comfortable leather sofas that had been placed to make the most of the view. 'How old are you, Ellie?'

She frowned. 'You really do have this thing about age, don't you?'

'Ellie?' His voice was weary and she shrugged and settled herself on the sofa opposite him.

'I'm forty-three,' she said cheerfully, and then subsided as she caught the look in his eyes. 'Well, I will be in twenty years' time. You're wondering how I've aged so well?'

'I'm wondering how you've survived twenty-three years without someone trying to strangle you,' he drawled. 'Tell me, what methods do people usually use to stop you talking?'

'Well, you could kiss me,' she suggested cheekily. 'That's bound to work.' Her smile faded as she saw the look in his eyes. 'OK, maybe not.'

The mere thought of being kissed by him sent her pulse rate soaring and she cursed Lindsay and moved quickly to a safer topic.

'So how do you know Uncle Jack?'

'I thought you just promised not to talk?'

'I promise to keep the subject matter neutral.' She slipped off her shoes and curled her legs under her on the sofa. 'You don't mind me making myself comfortable, do you?'

'I'm getting used to it. Just as long as you don't start removing your clothes.'

For a breath-stealing moment their gazes collided and she felt unusually flustered.

Perhaps he noticed because he broke the contact and stretched his long legs out in front of him, his eyes returning to the lake. 'How do I know Jack? Everyone knows Jack. The climbing community is pretty small, as you know. He's running a fantastically successful outfit here.'

Ellie nodded and finished her coffee. 'Yes, he's expanded a lot.'

Ben glanced towards her. 'Who are his clients? Is it mostly corporate stuff? Team-building for companies?'

'Well, that's certainly where the money is,' Ellie observed, nestling deeper into the sofa, 'but he takes other groups as well. Schoolchildren, people with disabilities—and he coaches climbers, of course.'

'And you help out?'

She laughed softly. 'When I have the time, which isn't very often, I'm afraid. Between the MRT and working in A and E, I don't have time for much else.' She bent to give Max a pat. 'My entire life is emergency medicine and the mountains, and the two of them are usually combined.'

'Sean mentioned that you were with the Mountain Rescue Team.' He gave a wry smile. 'I suppose I should have guessed that you would be, knowing your predilection for risk and danger. I suppose you do extreme skiing as a hobby, or maybe white-water rafting?'

Ellie chuckled and wrapped her hands around the warm mug. 'It isn't that risky. If you're a climber, you should know that.' She took another sip of coffee. 'And, anyway, I have a clever dog with me. He keeps me out of mischief.'

'I should think it would take more than a dog to do that.' Ben looked at the dog. 'How old is he?'

'Four. I've had him since he was a puppy. His daddy is Sean's dog. They bred him and were given a puppy from the litter. Ally decided that they couldn't cope with another dog and three children, so they offered him to me. Jack helped me train him and he passed his first assessment as a search dog last year.'

They talked about Max's training and then Ben glanced around him. 'These cabins are fantastic.'

'Yes.' Ellie smiled. 'For most of the summer they're booked out, but in the winter there's often a spare one or two and Uncle Jack lends them to friends.'

'But you live here all year round?'

She nodded. 'The cabin next door belongs to me. My dad set up this whole place with Jack.' She hesitated, the hand tickling the dog's ears suddenly still. 'My dad was a climber. He was killed climbing Everest.'

'I know who your dad was.' Ben's voice was soft, his dark gaze disturbingly intense. 'Sean told me.'

'You'd heard of him?'

'Are you serious?' Ben gave a wry smile. 'Phil Harrison was a legend in the climbing community.'

'I know that,' Ellie said proudly. 'He was the best.'

'Sean says you were with him when he climbed Everest.'

She nodded slowly. 'I trekked to Base Camp twice.'

'I can't believe he took you with him.'

'He took me everywhere,' Ellie said simply. 'It was just him and me, you see. Mum died when I was six months old and that meant that Dad either had to give up climbing, leave me at home or take me with him. He refused to contemplate the first two options so he took me with him. It was just a way of life to me. I never knew anything different.'

'Who looked after you when he was climbing?'

'There were always other people with us. They were my surrogate family.'

'It sounds like a pretty good childhood to me.'

'It was brilliant.' She stood still for a moment, a far-away look in her eyes, and then she pulled herself together. 'I wouldn't change any of it, except that I wish he hadn't made a summit push that day he died. A cornice collapsed and he was caught in an avalanche. They never found his body.'

There was a long silence and she was aware of the intensity of Ben's gaze.

'I'm sorry.'

Ellie gave a wan smile. 'When they told me about the avalanche, I refused to believe them. I wanted to climb up that mountain and dig him out with my bare hands. He'd always seemed invincible. I couldn't believe I wasn't going to see him again.' She shook herself slightly. 'Anyway, enough of that or I'll get maudlin.'

'I suppose knowing that you're his daughter explains a great deal.'

Her eyes widened. 'Like what?'

'Well, for a start, your passion for adventure,' he said dryly, and Ellie smiled.

'Yes, I suppose I do get that from him but, you know, the funny thing is, Dad never took risks. Not really.' She frowned slightly. 'He always said that the important thing was to know your own limits and not exceed them. But he also believed in living life to the full, and making the most of every day in case it was the last.' She stared pensively into her mug. 'I suppose that came from losing my mum when I was born. They loved each other very much.'

'And now you live your life the same way,' he commented, 'except maybe that your assessment of risk is slightly less astute than his.'

She glared at him. 'If you're talking about the ford again, I can assure you that it was safe. I've driven through it before.'

He lifted a hand to cut her off. 'Don't tell me. The mere thought horrifies me.'

Ellie laughed and finished her coffee. 'Do you know that old Tibetan saying? That it's better to live one day as a tiger than a lifetime as a...' She frowned. 'Oh, I can't remember what the alternative was supposed to be, but it was something terribly boring. Well, Dad was always telling me that. Instead of bedtime stories, I had real-life climbing stories. ''Don't be afraid, Ellie,'' he used to say. ''Fear stops us living our lives to the full. Whatever needs to be done, just go out there and do it.'''

'He was a brilliant climber and a very charismatic personality. It must have been very hard for you when he died.'

'It was hard,' she agreed, 'but I have so many good memories I suppose that makes me luckier than many. And I had an incredibly exciting childhood. My earliest memory is of brushing snow off my sleeping bag in the Alps. I always loved being outdoors with my dad.'

'And who looked after you after the accident?'

'Well, to begin with I lived with my aunt and uncle and Lindsay—that's why we're so close,' she explained, 'but when I reached eighteen and did my training, they decided I needed my own space so they let me choose the cabin I wanted and it's been mine ever since.'

'And do you climb much now?'

She tickled Max's ears. 'Only with the team. I'm not going to climb Everest if that's what you're asking. What about you?'

He seemed to hesitate and it was obvious that he was wary about revealing anything about himself. 'I just spent two years in Pakistan.'

'Climbing?'

'For some of the time.' His dark eyes were slightly veiled. 'I was part of an expedition to K2.'

'And did you make the summit?'

There was a strange light in his eyes. 'Yes.'

'Wow.' She stared at him with genuine admiration. K2 was the second highest mountain in the world and considered by many to be a more dangerous climb than Everest. 'My dad climbed K2.'

'Ellie, your dad climbed virtually everything.' He gave a soft laugh and she nodded proudly.

'Yes, he did.' She looked contemplative. 'So when did you come back?'

'A week ago.'

'You were working there as a doctor?'

Ben nodded. 'After I climbed K2 I was offered the chance to help set up a medical centre in one of the remote villages. I was involved in a research project on AMS— acute mountain sickness—and I helped out by staffing the clinic.'

'Right.' She looked at him steadily. 'Two years. That seems like a long time to be away from home.'

She sensed immediately that they were back to forbidden territory.

He was suddenly very still and she sensed the tension in his muscles. 'That's enough, Ellie.'

Ouch. Whatever was wrong, he really, really didn't want to talk about it.

'I'm sorry. I know I talk too much, but I only want to help.' She sprang to her feet and gave him a dazzling smile. 'Max and I need a walk so we'll be off. If you need anything, don't forget we're just next door.'

It wasn't just the dog that needed some fresh air, she reflected as she walked briskly along the footpath that led away from the cabins. She did, too. Either fresh air or a cold shower. Ben MacAllister was the most stunningly attractive man she'd ever laid eyes on and she was thinking thoughts she'd never even believed she was capable of.

And she was worried about him.

*   *   *

Ben paced around his cabin like a caged predator.

She was afraid he might forget she was next door?

He wished it was that easy.

The way he was feeling at the moment, he would have given quite a lot to forget Ellie.

Every time he turned round she seemed to be there, warm, smiley and incredibly sensitive to his every mood.

Was she a mind-reader?

He'd always prided himself on the ability to mask his feelings from others, and yet she seemed to see right through his armour of self-control to the pain he kept so tightly within himself.

Ben raked long fingers through his newly cropped hair and felt the tension ache in his shoulders.

He'd never met anyone quite like Ellie before. She was the total opposite of him.

Open, straightforward and very, very trusting.

And he clearly needed to work harder at hiding his feelings when he was near her. If he was on the receiving end of any more of her sweet sympathy he just might be tempted to forget all his resolutions about not becoming involved with a woman.

CHAPTER FOUR

'ELLIE are you listening to a word I'm saying?'

Ellie jumped and looked at her cousin. 'Sorry, Linny. What?'

'You're miles away!' Lindsay looked at her with amusement. 'Why bother visiting me if you're in cloud-cuckoo-land. What's happened? Have you won the lottery?'

No. She was thinking about Ben and wondering what he was hiding.

'Sorry. I was dreaming.'

'I noticed.' Lindsay gave her a wry look. 'Well, wake up and pay me some attention, please. Visiting is over in another half an hour and you've been cuddling those chocolates since you arrived. They'll all have melted if you don't give them to me soon.'

Ellie gasped and looked down at the box in her lap. 'Oh, Linny! I forgot about them.'

'I know.' Lindsay reached out and took them from her with a smile. 'You've been clutching them like a life raft since you walked in. And what I want to know is, what is about to sweep you away?' She grinned wickedly. 'Or should I say who?'

Ellie gave a guilty start. 'I don't know what you mean.'

'Ellie, this is me you're talking to,' Lindsay reminded her patiently. 'And, anyway, you know there's no point in you trying to hide your feelings. You burst if you even try.'

Ellie laughed. 'Am I that obvious?'

'Fortunately, yes.' Lindsay settled herself more comfortably and peeped into the cot by the bed to make sure that the baby was still asleep. 'Did you get your car fixed?'

Ellie nodded, still miles away. 'It was no problem.'

Lindsay stared at her impatiently. 'So, go on. Tell Aunty Lindsay.'

'I'm the aunty around here,' Ellie reminded her. 'Talking of which, I wish she'd wake up so I can have a cuddle.'

'Ellie…' Lindsay's tone warned that she didn't intend to be distracted but Ellie made a last attempt to divert her.

'Did you get any sleep last night?'

'Ellie!'

'Oh, all right.' Ellie sighed and rested her chin on her palm. 'You remember that doctor from last night?'

Lindsay pulled a face. 'Well, let me see—was that the guy who virtually saved both our lives? I think I have a dim recollection.'

'If you're going to be sarcastic then I'm going home,' Ellie warned, and Lindsay subsided.

'Sorry. Go on. I'm dying to hear everything.'

'There isn't much to tell,' Ellie confessed, 'except that it turns out that he's working in A and E for the next few months as a locum consultant and your dad has let him the cabin next to mine.'

Lindsay gave a whoop of delight and then clapped a hand over her mouth as the baby snuffled in the cot. 'That's fantastic,' she whispered, and Ellie sighed.

'No, it isn't. He thinks I'm reckless and that I talk too much.'

'You are and you do.' Lindsay shrugged. 'So?'

'Well, he isn't interested in me.'

He'd only let her cook breakfast because she'd given him no choice.

Lindsay stared at her. 'I wouldn't be so sure. What about you? Are you interested?'

Ellie bit her lip. 'I don't know…'

Ben was unlike any other men she'd ever met before.

'You can't be telling me you don't find him attractive?'

'Of course I find him attractive!' Ellie struggled to keep her voice low so that they wouldn't wake the baby. 'There's nothing wrong with my eyes! But looks aren't important to me, you know that. I'm not that shallow.' Or at least, she hoped she wasn't. But she had to admit that being near Ben did strange things to her body. She bit her lip, troubled by the way she felt. 'And I'm worried about him. I know there's something wrong.'

Lindsay opened the chocolates. 'What do you mean, there's something wrong?'

Ellie hesitated, reluctant to tell Lindsay what had happened. Ben was so intensely private that she didn't want to reveal his secret to anyone. 'I've just got one of my feelings.'

Lindsay rolled her eyes. 'Oh, heaven help the man, then. Where do these feelings stem from?'

Ellie bit her lip. 'He's been in Pakistan for *two whole years*. Don't you think that's odd?'

'Not particularly. He's a climber.'

Ellie frowned, 'True. But he's also a doctor, and a real hotshot according to Sean.' She helped herself to a chocolate and chewed slowly. 'Why would someone like that take themselves off to Pakistan for such a long time? Trust me, Lindsay, there's something wrong.'

'Well, just remember that not everyone likes to talk about their problems.'

'It's not healthy to bottle things up,' Ellie said firmly, and Lindsay sighed.

'Ellie, just seduce the man. That way, if he has got problems, at least you'll take his mind off them.'

Seduce him?

Ellie stared at her. 'But I've never seduced anyone in my life before.'

'I know.' Lindsay's tone was dry. 'That's why I suggested it. He's gorgeous, Ellie. Go for it.'

'He thinks I talk too much.'

'He's right. Next time you feel like talking, kiss him instead and see what happens.'

'I know what would happen. He'd give me one of his disapproving stares. Lin, I don't think he likes me!'

'He likes you.' Lindsay smiled placidly. 'Why else would he care whether you get swept away down river or abducted by a stranger? He likes you. Now you just need to persuade him to kiss you.'

'I'm really not sure I want him to kiss me.'

She had a feeling she might never recover.

Lindsay stared at her. 'Please, tell me you're joking. Ben MacAllister is a seriously sexy, tough, macho guy and *you don't want to kiss him*? Are you ill? You kiss everyone.'

Ellie blushed. 'Well, yes, but *not like that*.'

Even thinking about being kissed by Ben MacAllister made her feel strange. Sort of hot and panicky inside. Which was utterly ridiculous, she told herself briskly, because she'd been kissed plenty of times before. But only ever by men—*boys really*—her own age.

She knew instinctively that Ben was different. There was nothing boyish about Ben. He was one hundred per cent fully grown male, tough and self-confident.

Kissing him wouldn't be a harmless, childish experiment.

She knew instinctively that if Ben kissed a woman, it would be leading somewhere else.

'All right, everyone, we're bursting at the seams as usual so let's get started.' Sean looked at the whiteboard, his mouth grim as he looked at the number of patients. 'There was a nasty RTA on the motorway an hour ago, so Resus is full. Will, you go and see if they need any help. Ben, I need you to stay out here. If any more emergencies come in, they'll have to be dealt with in the corridor or the trolley bay. We've got two waiting for admission to the orthopaedic ward and I'm going to ring them to hurry them along. Nicky, what about nursing staff?'

'I've still got Laura and Polly in Resus with the RTA, so maybe Ellie should stay out here with Ben and you can put any emergencies in the trolley bay until we've cleared Resus,' the A and E sister said promptly. 'Chessie, you're in the treatment room, Alice in Theatre and the others can float.'

'OK, let's see if we can clear some space in this department,' Sean said briskly, 'and in the meantime let's hope we have a few hours peace and quiet.'

They didn't.

As Sean strode down the corridor to sort out the transfer of patients, the ambulance hotline rang and Ellie, dressed in blue theatre scrubs, her dark hair secured neatly in a ponytail, picked it up immediately.

She listened while ambulance control outlined the details of the patients they were bringing in, scribbling notes on her pad. Then she hung up and looked at Ben.

'Mother and son, complaining of headache and vomiting. No more details than that unfortunately.'

Ben lifted an eyebrow. 'ETA?'

'Two minutes.'

Even as she said the words they heard the siren and both of them sprinted towards the ambulance bay.

Ellie glanced surreptitiously at Ben, looking for signs of the tension that he'd shown on the first night, but he seemed relaxed and totally in control.

Maybe he'd been telling her the truth.

Maybe there really wasn't anything wrong.

The paramedic opened the doors and nodded to Ellie. 'They're in a bad way. The milkman called us because the curtains were drawn and he saw them lying on the floor. Might be a virus but it looks like something more than that to me. We've given them oxygen. Do you want them in Resus?'

'No. It's full. We're still dealing with the RTA victims. Take them through to the trolley bay for now.' She looked at Ben. 'I'll go and arrange another team to deal with the child and bleep Paeds.'

He gave a brief nod and she hurried off, joining them again as they wheeled the first stretcher into the trolley bay.

Ben immediately took charge, drawing the curtains round the trolley as he spoke. 'Mrs Bates, I'm Dr MacAllister. Can you tell me what happened?'

She gave a groan and opened her eyes with difficulty. 'Drowsy,' she murmured, lifting a hand to her head and wincing slightly. 'Terrible headache.'

Ben frowned. 'Since when?'

There was a long pause. 'Don't know,' she mumbled finally. 'I was all right last night but it was really cold so we cuddled in the sitting room. Headache…'

'We'll give you something for that in a minute.' Ben watched her keenly while the paramedics transferred her from their stretcher to the trolley. 'So, if you were fine last night, when did you start to feel ill?'

He was examining her as he spoke, searching for clues as to what could be wrong.

'I turned the heater on,' she said slowly, 'and we both just fell asleep in front of the fire. Then suddenly Tom woke up complaining of a headache and was sick everywhere.'

As if suddenly remembering her child, she gave a moan of anguish and roused herself with difficulty. 'Is he all right? Tom?'

'He'll be fine,' Ben said calmly. 'Another doctor is see-

ing to him right now. Let's worry about you for a moment.
Have you had the heater on before?'

Ellie stared at him in surprise, thinking that it was rather
a strange question. Why was he interested in her heater?

'The heater…' Mrs Bates closed her eyes and tried to
think. 'No. First time…this winter.' Her speech was
slurred, as if she could hardly stay awake. 'The central
heating boiler broke down and we haven't had it fixed yet.
It's a very old gas fire but it worked fine last winter. Oh,
help.' She gave a groan and lifted a hand to her mouth.
'I'm going to be sick.'

Ellie held a bowl for her while she vomited weakly and
Ben glanced up.

'Give her 100 per cent oxygen with a tight-fitting mask
and a reservoir bag and start an ECG. What's her blood
pressure?'

'Seventy over fifty,' Ellie said quickly, knowing that it
was a very low reading. 'Shall I set up the pulse oximeter
so that we can check her sats?'

Ben shook his head. 'It gives an incorrect reading in
carbon monoxide poisoning, which is what I suspect we're
dealing with here. Let's check her blood gases and the
carboxyhaemoglobin level and someone bleep the medical
reg.'

He turned back to the patient, his dark eyes serious.
'Could your heater be faulty, Mrs Bates?'

She swallowed with difficulty, her eyes exhausted. 'My
heater?'

Ben nodded. 'You're showing signs of carbon monoxide
poisoning. I suspect that you and Tom fell asleep and
breathed in carbon monoxide. You were lucky that you
woke up when you did.'

'Faulty heater?' Mrs Bates stared at him in dismay.
'Will it hurt the baby?'

Ben went still. 'You're pregnant?'

She nodded weakly. 'Four months. Oh, no...' She started to sob quietly. 'Don't tell me this will have hurt the baby. Please.'

'Try not to worry.' Ben gave her hand a squeeze and then lifted his gaze to Ellie. 'Call the Poisons Information Centre. Ask them for the whereabouts of the nearest hyperbaric oxygen unit.'

Ellie hurried to the phone and was back minutes later with the information.

'That's less than an hour by ambulance,' Ben said tersely as he finished taking the necessary bloods. 'Can you arrange transport? We need to get her there as fast as possible. If you sort out the ambulance I'll call the consultant and set up an escort.'

'I've already done it,' Ellie said immediately. 'They'll be here in five minutes.'

Ben blinked. 'Well done.' He smiled briefly and Ellie felt warmth spread through her insides. It felt surprisingly good to be praised by him.

She risked another look at him but there was no sign of the tension that had affected him so badly yesterday.

Maybe he'd just been tired.

She waited while Ben wrote a letter to go with the patient and then helped her into the ambulance, along with the son.

'How was the son doing?' she asked Ben as they watched the ambulance pull away, blue light flashing.

'All right, according to Sean.'

'Thank goodness they have their milk delivered. Imagine if no one had seen them. They would have died.' Ellie wrapped her arms around her middle and gave a shiver as the cold winter air oozed through the thin fabric of her theatre pyjamas. 'Can I ask you something?'

'Of course.' He turned to face her, his expression patient.

'What made you think it might be carbon monoxide poisoning? I've never seen it before,' Ellie confessed. 'I thought one of the signs is that the patient is cherry red, but she was really pale.'

He nodded. 'Cherry-red colouring of the skin is actually very rare in live patients. It's sometimes seen in fatal carbon monoxide poisoning.'

Ellie digested that piece of information. 'And why hyperbaric oxygen for her and not the child?'

'Because, although it sounds logical, there's actually no proven benefit after carbon monoxide poisoning and it's often difficult to care for a critically ill patient in a small chamber,' he told her. 'However, she's pregnant, which makes a difference. I've spoken to the consultant at the hospital and he's going to assess her when she arrives.'

'Oh.' Ellie was impressed by the depth of Ben's knowledge.

There was a hint of amusement in his dark eyes as he looked at her expectantly. 'Anything else?'

There were hundreds of things she wanted to ask him. *Like how did he always know what to do in any given situation?*

'Will she be all right? Will she have problems in the future?'

He breathed out heavily. 'That's harder to answer. Some patients develop neurological and psychiatric problems a few weeks after poisoning but they usually settle down.'

'Oh. Well, I hope so.' Ellie smiled up at him. 'You were brilliant. There seemed to be no clues when they were admitted but within minutes you knew exactly what was wrong with them.'

Ben shrugged dismissively. 'A and E medicine is often a bit like detective work. Doctors in other specialities usually get a history, we just get a patient and have to guess from the symptoms. But there are always clues. It's just a question of spotting them. Now, let's go back inside before we both freeze.'

Ellie walked with him back into the unit, thinking that he was obviously an extremely clever man.

Clever and disturbingly attractive.

The department was full to bursting all day and it was towards the end of the afternoon when Ellie's pager went off.

Ben looked at her as they finished stitching a patient who'd fallen through a plate-glass window. 'Is that a call-out?'

Ellie looked at the pager and nodded. 'They need a dog team up on the fells. I've got to rendezvous at the Drunken Fox in twenty minutes.'

'Then you'd better go.'

'I'll just do the tetanus injection,' Ellie said quickly. 'You really ought to see your GP and get the rest of your immunisations up to date,' she told the patient, moving over to the trolley and snapping the top of the relevant ampoule.

Ben was concentrating on the wound. 'Will you tell Sean?'

'He'll already know. Jack always tells him when there's a call-out because he knows it could present a staffing problem.' She moved over to the patient, gave the injection quickly and smiled apologetically at Ben. 'Is it OK if I leave you to it? You've nearly finished and I've got to pull on some suitable gear.'

Ben stitched with a speed and skill that made her blink. 'What about Max?'

'Jack will bring him and I always carry my gear in the car just in case.' Ellie threw the remains of the ampoule into the sharps bin and glanced at her watch. 'I'm virtually at the end of my shift anyway. I'd better tell Nicky…'

She turned to walk to the office but Nicky and Sean were already on their way towards her.

Sean's expression told Ellie that he already knew what was happening. 'I've just spoken to Jack. The police have had a call from two walkers. One of them slipped, crossing a waterfall, and he's injured. They tried to take a short cut and now they're lost. The mist has come down, it's going to be dark in an hour. He's sending up one section of the MRT and one dog team. You and Max.'

'Then I'd better get a move on, if that's all right with you?' Ellie looked at Nicky who smiled and nodded.

'Of course it is. Be careful.'

At that moment Ben joined them, his expression curious as he saw them gathered in a huddle.

Sean's gaze flickered to his friend. 'Just the person. Ben, he wants a doctor, too, so I said you'd do it.'

Ben gave a brief nod. 'No problem. I'll pick up my gear and meet them there.'

Ben was joining them? Ellie felt a moment of surprise. There was a waiting list to join the Mountain Rescue Team and a huge amount of training and assessment involved. Still, Ben was obviously an incredibly skilled climber and the politics of the rescue team wasn't any of her business. And he already seemed to know almost everyone so maybe it wasn't really surprising.

She sprinted to her car, grabbed her gear and returned to the staffroom to change. Quickly she pulled on thermal underwear, fleecy top and trousers and stuffed her theatre pyjamas into the laundry bin.

Then she scooped up her dark hair and stuffed it under a fleece hat. It was going to be bitterly cold out there and she wanted to make sure that she was prepared.

Saying a quick goodbye to Sean, she hurried back to her car and drove quickly to the rendezvous point at the Drunken Fox.

Jack was already there with the other members of the team, staring at a map. He looked up with a grin as Ellie struggled in with her rucksack and waterproof gear. 'What took you so long?'

Ellie slung the gear onto the floor. 'Oh, you know, filing my nails, blow drying my hair—all the usual girly things. Got to look good before I go up a mountain in a gale-force wind. You never know who you might meet.'

Max bounded up to her, tail wagging, and she stooped to hug him.

'OK.' Jack turned his attention back to the map and stabbed it with the end of his pen. 'Their last known position was here, but they walked for at least half an hour after that so we guess they're now about here.' He tapped the map again. 'They called us on a mobile and Base are going to stay in touch with them and keep us informed. There are two of them and one of them is injured, we don't know how badly.'

Ted Wilson, the equipment officer, pulled a face. 'It would be good to have a doctor on this one. Where's Sean?'

'Busy,' Jack said tersely, 'but I've got someone else just as good, if not better.'

At that moment the door opened again and Ben walked in, his powerful presence immediately dominating the room.

'Jack.' Unsmiling, he gave a brief nod of acknowledgement and walked over to join the group, his attention immediately on the map.

Ellie swallowed. He was devilishly good-looking and totally self-possessed. Unlike the other members of the group, Ben didn't chat or joke. Instead, he was silent and watchful, speaking when he had something to contribute and then only briefly.

But when he did speak, everyone fell silent, listening

intently, as if there was something about Ben that set him apart from other men.

And there was.

He had the strength and confidence of a natural leader and Ellie realised at once why Jack had asked Ben to join them.

You only had to look at the respect in the eyes of the rest of the team members to understand that they considered it a privilege to work with him.

Jack glanced round the group. 'OK, folks, this is the plan.' He outlined where the search would take place and tapped the map again. 'We'll search in pairs over this area. Be warned that the weather forecast is poor.'

Ted's eyes narrowed. 'How poor?'

'Gale-force winds.'

Ted rolled his eyes. 'I'm so glad I asked.'

'We've got Ellie and Max, and if the storm is bad we'll need them,' Jack continued. 'We all know that a dog is equivalent to twenty searchers in good conditions and we're not going to have good conditions so they're an essential part of the team. Ellie, I want you to search four hundred metres behind Ben and me.'

Ellie nodded and started pulling on her waterproof jacket and trousers. Once she was ready she started on Max, slipping him into his high-visibility jacket which also had bells and a green chemical light fastened to it so that she could hear and see him in poor weather conditions.

As they left the pub she winced slightly as the wind buffeted her madly. And they hadn't even reached any height yet. What was the weather going to be like up the top?

It was dark within an hour and Ellie stayed on the path, battling to stay upright in the appalling wind. If it hadn't been for the heavy pack on her back, she was sure that she would have been blown off the mountain.

In contrast, Max seemed totally indifferent to the weather, using the wind to his advantage as he searched for human scent.

Finally she reached the location where the walkers were believed to be. Ben and Jack were already there, and Jack was on the radio to the Mountain Rescue Team base.

'Bad news.' Jack tucked the radio away and adjusted the neck of his jacket. 'The battery in their cellphone has just died so now we have no contact whatsoever. They're not where they thought they were, so what we have here is a very serious incident. I've called out the rest of the MRT and another search dog team.'

As the others caught up Ellie squinted through the darkness up the path.

'If he slipped, crossing the waterfall back there, and then walked on, then they would be further than this.'

'Or maybe they didn't read their map properly,' Ben suggested quietly, 'and this isn't the right stream.'

Jack looked at him. 'What are you saying?'

'Well, looking at the map, it would be fairly easy to make a mistake.' Ben planted his legs firmly apart to brace himself against the wind as he studied the map again with Jack.

Ellie peered round his shoulder at the map. 'But the other stream isn't far away. Max and I could go on.'

Jack shook his head immediately. 'No way. The weather is too bad for the two of you to be searching on your own now.'

'But what she says makes sense,' Ben said. 'We do need to check further on as well as down here. I'll go with her and you carry on down this path.'

Jack nodded. 'All right. Stay in contact.'

Ben turned to Ellie, his voice raised to make himself

heard above the storm. 'Follow a compass bearing of 280,' he shouted, 'and stay behind me.'

She nodded to show that she'd understood and he immediately strode off, leaving her to walk quickly if she was to catch up.

Grumbling about the length of her legs, she struggled along the boggy ground on a new search pattern.

After about two hundred metres Ellie heard something and reached out to grab Ben's arm.

He stopped immediately, his eyes narrowed against the vicious wind. 'What?'

'I heard something,' she yelled. 'Listen…'

They both stood still but heard nothing but the howling wind, and she frowned and looked around for Max. Where was he?

Finally she saw his little light appearing and disappearing as he quartered the boggy ground in his search for human scent.

Suddenly she saw him stop and prick up his ears.

Ellie shouted encouragement to the dog and then heard the distinct noise of a distress whistle as the light attached to the dog's coat vanished into the darkness.

Gesturing to Ben that they should follow him, she walked quickly after Max and then heard barking.

Ben turned to her as they walked. 'He's found them?' he asked in amazement.

Ellie shook her head. 'That's not Max. A search dog never barks at the body. Only at the handler. The walkers must have a dog with them.'

'Or maybe it isn't them.'

But Max reappeared out of the mist and threw himself at Ellie, barking and jumping up until she was covered in wet mud.

'Good boy.' She laughed, pushing him away as he threatened to knock her right over. 'Clever dog.'

They walked a few more strides and saw the walkers, huddled together by a rock, looking mightily relieved to see them.

Ellie made a fuss of Max and turned to look at Ben. 'He's found them.' Brisk and professional, she picked up her radio. 'I'll give Jack our position while you give them the once-over.'

Ben was looking at her with a strange look in his eyes. 'You're a different person up here. I'm impressed.'

Suddenly he smiled and because it was so unusual to see him smile she was utterly captivated for a moment. The harshness of his features softened and he looked a hundred times more approachable. Then the smile was gone and he was shrugging the pack off his back and focusing on the task in hand—assessing the injuries and deciding on the best course of action.

Dragging her gaze away from his broad shoulders, Ellie called Jack and then sent up a flare to indicate their position before returning to help Ben with the climbers. He was on his knees, running a hand over the man's injured leg, questioning him about exactly what had happened.

'We lost the path in the mist and when we crossed the waterfall I slipped. Completely stupid of me, I know.' He pulled a face and looked thoroughly embarrassed. 'To be honest, if there'd been any way of getting myself off the mountain without calling you guys out then I would have done it, but my leg's a mess. Once we saw how bad it was, we called you. Then the battery in the mobile died. We were beginning to think we were going to have to spend the night here, so we were mighty relieved to see your dog.'

Ellie dropped to her knees beside him and looked at Ben. 'What's the damage?'

'Compound fracture of his tib and fib,' Ben said immediately. 'Is Jack carrying a vacuum splint?'

Ellie nodded. 'Yes. Sean sent one over when they called in and described their injuries. He had a feeling it might be needed.'

'The man's clairvoyant.' Ben delved into his rucksack and pulled out a venflon and a giving set. 'I'm going to get a line in. Ellie, lay your hands on some sterile dressings so that we can cover this wound. And tell Jack to get some Entonox up here quickly. I need to give some pain relief while I fix this leg.'

Ellie glimpsed white bone poking out through the torn flesh and she knew that it needed to be covered to try and minimise the risk of infection.

Ben was explaining what he was doing to the injured walker. 'You've fractured a bone in your lower leg. I'm going to bring it back into alignment in a minute and then we'll put it in a splint and get you down the mountain to hospital.'

At that moment Jack and the rest of the team arrived and there was a flurry of activity while the necessary equipment was identified.

'OK, I've got a line in.' Ben taped the cannula to the man's hand and glanced expectantly at Ellie who immediately handed him the giving set attached to a bag of fluid, stunned by how quickly he worked. No wonder Jack had asked him to join them. He wasn't just good, he was awesome. 'Analgesia next and then I'll reduce that fracture.'

Ten minutes later the man's leg was safely protected by a sterile dressing and a splint and he was being lifted onto a stretcher.

Jack blinked. 'You certainly don't waste time, Ben, I'll give you that. Good job, guys.'

'Thank you.' Ellie's tone was sarcastic and Jack gave her a wink.

'You're one of the guys, Ellie, you know that.'

'You have a strange idea of what makes a compliment,'

Ellie grumbled as she checked the pulses in the injured man's foot and gave Ben a nod to indicate that everything was fine. She knew how important it was to check the circulation, but she also knew that their next priority was to get the man safely off the mountain as quickly as possible.

The man was in pain but still distinctly embarrassed. 'I never thought this would happen to me. Having to call out the rescue team…'

'Don't worry about it,' Jack said cheerfully. 'We all needed the exercise. You can buy me a pint when you're out of hospital.'

'How on earth are you going to carry me down the mountain?'

'We're not.' Jack's mouth twitched. 'That's the reason we bring Ellie. She looks small, but underneath all those waterproofs she's built like a weightlifter.'

Everyone laughed and they made the final preparations until Ben gave Jack a nod to indicate that they should start the descent.

'We'll take the stretcher.' Jack raised his voice to make himself heard above the wind. 'You walk with Ellie to make sure she's OK.'

As Ellie stood up a gust of wind punched her in the back, throwing her forward into Ben who was standing in front.

Instantly he clamped her against him, bracing himself to keep them both upright in the wind. He was all hard muscle and solid male strength and her sudden shiver had nothing to do with the cold. Her insides turned to liquid and she tipped her face up to his and stared hungrily at the firm outline of his mouth. The longing for him to kiss her was overwhelming. Her body was flooded with sensations that she'd never experienced before. She felt as though she was on the verge of something momentous. Something that would change her life.

For a moment they stared at each other, the tension between them heating the freezing air around them.

And then she saw Ben's mouth tighten and he released her so suddenly that she almost fell again.

'We need to get down,' he said roughly. 'You can barely stay upright in this wind. You go first. I'll stay behind you.' He avoided looking at her as he gathered up the equipment, shrugged his broad shoulders into the rucksack and started off down the path.

Struggling to contain her disappointment, Ellie zipped her jacket up firmly to keep out the wind and prepared herself for a difficult walk back down the mountain.

As they started the long trudge down the narrow path, Ellie was aware of Ben's reassuring bulk behind her.

What was he thinking?

Was he wishing that he'd kissed her?

Probably not, she thought miserably, or he would have done it. She scrambled over a rocky outcrop that blocked the path, her mind drifting. Maybe he didn't want to kiss her. Maybe she was reading the signals all wrong. After all, it was hardly her area of expertise. She could count the number of men she'd kissed in her life on one hand, and as for anything else…

She frowned as she picked her way over a particularly narrow bit of the path. She was sure that he *had* wanted to kiss her.

She had one of her feelings…

Trying to make sense of her tangled thoughts, she battled to stay upright in the wind, and when they finally reached the car park of the Drunken Fox she was exhausted.

They took the injured man across to the Mountain Rescue Team ambulance and two of the team transferred him to hospital. The rest of them made for the warm log fire in the pub.

'Not a bad rescue for a puny girl,' Jack teased as he ordered a round of drinks and some bacon rolls. 'And what the hell happened to you anyway?' He stared at the mud all over her jacket. 'You look as though you fell in a bog and as for the smell…!'

Ellie put her hands on her hips. 'I do not smell and I did not fall in a bog! Max was excited that he'd found the climbers and he threw himself at me.' Ellie's tone was indignant and then she saw subdued smiles all around and realised that she was being teased. 'You were great, too, Jack,' she said sweetly, her tone suddenly light. 'No one would ever suspect that you're a grandfather now.'

There was a chorus of whoops from the burly men gathered around the bar and Ellie pinned a concerned look on her face.

'Maybe you're getting a bit old to be climbing in the mountains.'

Jack glowered at her over his shoulder as he passed the drinks around. 'Watch yourself. You're not too old to put you over my knee, young lady.'

Ellie smiled. 'I love you, Uncle Jack.'

Jack glared. 'Don't you "Uncle Jack" me.'

'You've got to develop a sense of humour now you're a grandfather,' she said primly, and Jack looked helplessly at Ben.

'What would you do with her?'

Ben's firm mouth moved slightly. 'You don't want to know.'

Ellie's heart missed a beat as her eyes met his and she looked away quickly, hoping that he couldn't read her mind. She knew what she wanted him to do with her, but it was too much to hope for that he'd want the same thing. *She didn't get that lucky.*

*   *   *

He could read her like a book.

Ben watched Ellie at the bar, being teased by men twice her age and size, chuckling at something Jack had said, her cheeks dimpling prettily and her green eyes brimming with laughter. The Mountain Rescue Team seemed to treat her as some sort of mascot, and yet he'd seen respect in their eyes. And it was well deserved. Her performance during the rescue had been amazing. She barely reached his shoulder and yet she'd walked over difficult ground in treacherous weather conditions with her usual cheerful smile.

As he drained his glass he noticed that several of the other men in the bar were watching her with interest, and it was hardly surprising. She was gorgeous and totally unaware of the impact that she had on men.

In fact, the only man he'd seen her show interest in was himself.

Which was a shame, he thought grimly as he finished his drink and put the empty glass back on the bar. Because he had no intention of pursuing her, despite the temptation.

And the temptation was strong.

He'd come close to kissing her earlier on the mountain and it had taken all his will-power to pull back.

He could still remember the slender softness of her body as she'd leaned against him for support.

Damn.

Ben straightened abruptly and gathered up his gloves and rucksack.

Aware that she was still looking at him, only a rigid self-control, well developed over the years, prevented him from losing himself in those amazing eyes before dragging her home and doing exactly what he knew they both wanted.

But he was an incredibly self-disciplined man and he knew he couldn't afford to let that control slip. Not even for a moment. It would be cruel because he wouldn't be good for Ellie. How could he be, after everything that had happened?

And she wouldn't be good for him.

He gave a harsh laugh as he was forced to ask himself exactly who he was protecting. Ellie or himself?

He'd learned to keep part of himself detached from women but he sensed that with Ellie that rigid self-control could be severely tested.

And he wasn't going to take that risk.

CHAPTER FIVE

THE freezing weather continued and A and E was the busiest it had been for months.

'Someone should market this as a diet,' Nicky complained one morning as she rubbed her stomach. 'I've lost half a stone in the last two weeks because I never have time for coffee, lunch or tea. I'm calling it the NHS diet. We replace meals with work. It's foolproof.'

Ellie glanced up and nodded as she sorted through a pile of X-rays. 'I know what you mean.'

Everyone was the same. There were too many patients and not enough staff, and they frequently worked through without breaks. Tempers were frayed and everyone was tired.

'Maybe we could persuade the police to issue a statement, asking everyone to stay indoors,' Will suggested as they hurried to greet yet another ambulance. 'If they're indoors, they don't slip on the ice.'

'No, they fall downstairs or scald themselves,' Ellie reminded him cheerfully. 'Accidents in the home—remember? It's a lethal place to be.'

She was reminded of her words later when Ambulance Control rang to say that they were bringing in a child with severe scalds.

Ellie replaced the phone and hurried to find Ben. She found him in one of the cubicles, checking an X-ray for one of the casualty officers. 'I need you in Resus.'

He gave a brief nod to show that he'd heard, finished talking to the more junior doctor and followed her through to Resus.

96

Was it her imagination or did he hesitate slightly in the doorway?

'What's the story?' He paced across the room and paused by the intubation tray, picking up a laryngoscope and checking the bulb.

'We don't know much. Just that it's a small child with burns.' She watched him closely, sensing that something was wrong.

He was staring at the laryngoscope in his hand as if it might jump up and bite him. Even as she watched, beads of sweat appeared on his brow and there was a change in his breathing.

So it hadn't been her imagination.

It was just like that first night, but why now when he'd been fine all week?

She chewed her lip and then her eyes widened as realisation dawned.

It was something to do with Resus.

'Oh!'

He looked up sharply, his fingers clenched on the laryngoscope. 'What's wrong?'

'Nothing,' she lied, knowing that this was certainly not the time to bring it up. What she needed to do was distract him from whatever feelings tormented him when he entered Resus. She thought quickly. 'I haven't seen many burns cases—when do you usually refer them to the burns unit?'

He was silent for a moment, his jaw rigid with tension, and then his grip on the laryngoscope relaxed and he placed it back on the tray.

'Anything over ten per cent of the body area,' he said finally, and she nodded, pleased that his voice sounded more or less normal.

'And one arm is about nine per cent?'

'That's right, but obviously with a child you need to use

their palm as an indication of surface area. And in children the head is relatively larger and the legs are relatively smaller.'

'Well, they said that this was a scald, so I suppose the severity depends on the temperature of the water,' she observed, straightening slightly as the doors crashed open and the paramedics hurried in, carrying a little girl who was crying miserably.

She cast a quick look at Ben but, just like the time before, once the patient was in the room he seemed to be back in control.

'This is Sophie Bassett. She pulled a kettle of boiling water over herself, but as far as we can see it's mostly her arm.' The paramedic quickly briefed Ben. 'The babysitter put it in cold water straight away so it could have been a lot worse. It's difficult to get a look at it because she's so upset.'

Ben nodded. 'Where's the mother?'

'Out, at a concert. Her aunt was babysitting, and she brought her in. She's giving all the details to Reception.'

Ben let out a long breath as he looked at the screaming child. 'OK, well can someone try and get hold of the mother quickly?' He glanced at Ellie and rubbed a hand over the back of his neck, the tension visible again. 'Will you try and hold her while I examine her?'

'Of course.' Without hesitation, Ellie scooped the child out of the arms of the paramedic and cuddled her close, careful to avoid the burn.

The little girl doubled her screams and Ellie winced slightly and racked her brains for a suitable distraction.

'Oh, my goodness!'

Her tone was urgent and both Ben and the paramedic looked at her with alarm. Even Sophie's sobs lessened.

'The train is leaving!' Ellie walked across to the trolley and took the brake off with her foot. 'We could have missed it, Sophie! If we hurry, we can just about catch it. Do you want to sit up front with the driver?'

Sophie's sobs had now stopped completely and she was looking at Ellie with round eyes, her thumb creeping up into her mouth.

'You can sit in the back if you like,' Ellie said briskly, 'but you'll have to decide quickly because the seats are filling up.'

Sophie mumbled round her thumb. 'In the fwont.'

Ellie gave an approving nod. 'Front it is. Good choice. This train is going to the seaside. Is that OK with you?'

Sophie nodded and Ellie placed her carefully on the trolley and made a train noise.

'Off we go. Now, then, this man…' She lifted her eyes and winked at Ben. 'This man is the conductor and he's going to give you a ticket.'

She tipped her head on one side and looked expectantly at Ben, who was clearly speechless. She prompted him gently. 'The ticket, Conductor?'

Ben blinked and then fumbled in his pocket before pulling out a piece of paper. 'Er—this?'

'Perfect. The trouble is, Sophie, the conductor can't sell you a ticket to the seaside until he's had a look at your arm. So can he do that now?'

Sophie hesitated and then nodded slowly.

'Good girl.' Ellie moved to the other side of the trolley so that she could be next to Ben. She carried on chatting to the little girl, noting that the skin was red and blistered.

Ben glanced up. 'Can we give her some paracetamol syrup for the pain?'

Ellie nodded, all her attention still focused on Sophie. 'Aren't you lucky? The conductor says you can have some of our special pink drink. I'll just fetch that for you now.'

She left the room to fetch the drug and when she re-

turned she stopped dead, astonished to see Ben and the
paramedic both making train noises.

Smothering a smile, she walked briskly across the room
and handed the little girl the tiny container. 'Sip this,
sweetheart, it will make you enjoy your trip more.'

Ben was examining the little girl, and Ellie felt a lump
in her throat as she saw how careful he was, his strong
fingers infinitely gentle as he assessed the severity of the
burn.

'Ellie, can we clean this up with some saline?'

She pulled herself together and ripped open a dressing
pack. 'I'm just going to make your arm more comfortable,
Sophie, and then put a bandage on it so that you don't get
sand in it when this train arrives at the beach.'

She cleaned the burn carefully, finding new distractions
every time the little girl's lip wobbled. At one point she
glanced uncertainly at Ben.

'Do you want me to aspirate that blister?'

Ben looked closely at it and shook his head. 'No. It
looks fine. It's not tense and it will protect the epithelium
underneath while it heals. Use some sulphadiazine cream
and jelonet.'

Ellie carefully did as he'd requested, astonished that the
little girl was being so brave. Then she applied the gauze
and an absorbent layer of cotton wool and held the whole
lot in place with a firm crêpe bandage.

'All right. That's good.' With a nod of satisfaction, Ben
took a step back from the trolley and picked up the little
girl's record card. 'We don't know her immunisation status
so we'll have to wait until her mum gets here to find out
if she needs a tetanus.'

At that moment Nicky entered the room, accompanied
by a woman who was clearly flustered and out of breath.

'Mrs Bassett?' Ellie walked over to her and the woman
nodded.

'Yes. I came as soon as I got the message. I can't believe this has happened.' She hurried over to Sophie who still had her thumb in her mouth.

'I'm on a twain,' Sophie mumbled, and her mother looked startled.

'What, darling?' She looked anxiously at Ben. 'Is it bad?'

He put down the notes he'd been filling in and slipped his pen into his pocket. 'Your daughter has a nasty scald to one arm,' he told her. 'It's very red and blistered but it doesn't seem to have affected the deep layers of skin so I'm confident that it will heal by itself in ten to fourteen days. We've given her some paracetamol—you can give her some more in four hours' time. Is she fully immunised?'

The mother nodded. 'Oh, yes, she's had everything she should have had.'

'Good.' Ben gave her a brief smile. 'In that case, you can take her home now and take her back to your GP in two days to have the dressing changed. Mrs Bassett, you need to think about shortening the flex on your kettle. Apparently she grabbed it and pulled the kettle over herself.'

The mother's eyes filled with tears. 'I left her with my sister—I can't believe she was in the kitchen unattended.'

'Accidents happen,' Ben said quietly, 'and your sister had the presence of mind to put her arm in cold water immediately. I have no doubt that her actions helped prevent the scald being more severe.'

He talked to her for a few more minutes before Ellie escorted them back to the reception area and then went back to Resus to clear up.

Ben was still writing up the notes but he glanced up as she walked in, his eyes warm.

'Ellie, you were really wonderful with that child.'

'Oh.' Pleased by his praise, she felt warmth flood through her veins. 'Thank you. Just luck really…'

'No.' Ben shook his head and gave a faint smile. 'It was inspired. I never would have thought of it. Without you I don't think she would have let me examine her.'

'Well, you're not that great as a conductor,' she joked. 'A bit slow off the mark, if you ask me. From now on carry some tickets in your pocket.'

'Maybe I'll do that.' His eyes held hers and her smile slowly faded, her whole body responding to the expression in his eyes.

And then suddenly the expression was gone and he straightened and checked his watch. 'Nearly time for us to call it a day.'

'Yes.' Her voice was croaky and she cleared her throat. 'Have you had anything at all to eat yet?'

'Of course not.' He gave a wry smile. 'Have you?'

She shook her head. 'Not since breakfast. A few of them are going for a pizza,' she told him, trying to keep her voice casual. 'Are you going?'

He shook his head and strolled towards the door. 'I'm off home.'

Ellie watched him go, trying to breathe slowly and calm her pulse rate.

When she was near him she felt excited, euphoric—*alive*. But when he left the room it was as if the whole world had gone dark.

What was happening to her?

'So who's coming across the road for dinner?'

There was a loud chorus of assent from everyone except Ellie, who shook her head and picked up her coat.

She'd made up her mind what she was going to do, and it didn't involve pizza.

'Not me. I promised I'd look in on Lindsay.' She hadn't

planned to do so, but it seemed a useful excuse and it was certainly better than saying that she wanted to see Ben.

She needed to be near him.

Was this what love felt like?

Still baffled by the strange feelings that were tumbling around inside her, she stopped briefly at Lindsay's house. She cuddled Storm, somehow managed to avoid all her cousin's awkward questions and then drove home via the supermarket. As she pulled up outside the cabins she noticed with a frown that Ben's was in darkness.

Had he gone out after all?

Remembering the chilly reception he'd given her when she'd cooked his breakfast, she hesitated before rapping lightly on his door, her fingers tightening on the carrier bag of food she'd picked up.

As the door opened she dived straight into the speech she'd prepared, not giving him time to protest.

'I came to invite you to supper. And I know you'll be angry but you haven't eaten all day and neither have I and it isn't good for us to go without food and don't say no because it's just supper,' she said, blurting the words out so quickly that he didn't have time to interrupt. 'You have to eat and I've bought us something so you don't have to bother. I can cook it at your place or mine. It doesn't matter which.'

He leaned his broad shoulders against the door-frame and a ghost of a smile flickered across his handsome face.

'Take a breath before you pass out.'

Ellie's eyes twinkled in response. 'I was afraid that if I paused for breath you'd say no.'

He looked at her quizzically. 'What happened to the pizza trip?'

She licked her lips. 'I decided not to go.'

'Why?'

Suddenly his gaze seemed unusually penetrating and she

dropped her eyes and rubbed her toe on the ground. 'Because I'd rather be with you.'

She heard the sharp intake of his breath.

'Ellie, what is going on here?' His voice was gentle and she looked up and blushed slightly as she met his eyes.

'I don't know. Believe me, it's very unsettling for me, too. I've never felt this way before. I don't understand it. I think it's very possible that I'm falling in love with you—but you don't need to panic,' she said quickly as she saw the dark frown appear. 'I know you don't feel the same way. You think I'm too young, I talk too much and I'm reckless. And you're probably right. Either way, I'm clearly not your type. And that's fine. It's my problem, not yours.'

'Ellie, trust me, you are not in love with me!' His tone was harsh and she pulled a face.

'I think I might be.'

He made an exasperated sound. 'You are not!'

'Now you're cross, which must mean you're hungry,' she began and he raked a hand through his dark hair and growled with frustration.

'Ellie, you can't come in and cook me dinner!'

'Why ever not?' She stared at him, puzzled, and then her face cleared. 'Oh, you mean because of what I said about possibly being in love with you? You needn't worry. I'm a very practical person. I promise that it won't affect the quality of my cooking.'

He groaned and stared heavenwards. 'Ellie, you're trying my patience—'

'That's because you're starving. *Please?*' She rustled the bag temptingly and her tone was coaxing. 'It's my speciality. Bolognese sauce with linguine.'

He glowered at her and then gave a sigh. 'What am I going to do with you?'

'Well, I know what I'd like you to do with me—but I

don't suppose there's much chance of that,' she added hastily as she saw his eyes darken. 'So how about you just invite me in and let me feed you?'

He breathed in deeply and shook his head. 'It really, really isn't a good idea.'

'Of course it is! We're both starving and I have the ingredients for a meal in my bag.'

'Ellie…'

She gave a sigh and tilted her head to one side. 'Ben, letting me cook you supper isn't going to change the way I feel. But if it embarrasses you to hear that I think I'm falling in love with you then I promise not to mention it again.'

'Ellie, you are *not* in love with me!'

She frowned at him, genuinely puzzled. 'I can't understand why it upsets you so much. Millions of women must have fallen for you over the years—surely you're used to it by now?'

He closed his eyes wearily. 'Ellie, it's just a crush.'

'Maybe…' She looked at him doubtfully. 'Let's hope so, shall we? So, now that we've got that straight, can I come in and start cooking? It takes half an hour and I'm starving.'

There was a long, painful silence and she was just resigning herself to being rejected when he breathed in sharply and straightened up.

'All right. On one condition.'

'Which is?'

'You don't talk me to death, or ask me questions I don't want to answer. And…' he paused for emphasis and his expression was stern '…as long as you give up this crazy notion that you're in love with me.'

'That's more than one condition,' she pointed out, 'and obviously I can't change the way I feel, but I can stop talking about it if it makes you uncomfortable.' She followed him through the door, talking over her shoulder. 'Can I put garlic in the sauce or will it frighten the patients?'

He gave a wry smile. 'Put it in. If we manage to frighten away a few patients, we might manage to take lunch-breaks.'

She washed her hands and opened the bags but he put out a hand and stopped her.

'It's my turn to cook.'

She stared at him stupidly. 'You?'

'Don't look at me like that.' He washed his hands and dried them. 'Men can cook, you know.'

He picked up a knife and chopped onion and garlic with a speed that made her jaw drop.

'Did you used to be a chef?'

'No, a surgeon. Plenty of practice with knives.'

She laughed and then settled herself on a stool to watch him cook. 'Lindsay sends her love, by the way. I called on my way home tonight. You're her hero.'

He frowned slightly, clearly uncomfortable with the thought. 'How's the baby doing?'

'Fine. She's gorgeous.' Ellie watched as he browned the meat and added the onions and garlic. 'Can I ask you something?'

'Here we go again.' He snapped open a tin of tomatoes. 'Knowing you, it will be something that most human beings wouldn't dare voice. You're the only person I've ever met who says exactly what's in her head without any censorship whatsoever.'

'Well, at least you know what I'm thinking,' she pointed out and he gave a short laugh.

'I suppose there is that. Go on, then. Ask away.'

'This thing that's upsetting you,' she said slowly, 'it's something to do with Resus, isn't it?'

The temperature in the room suddenly fell below zero and the expression in Ben's dark eyes was forbidding.

'Ellie—nothing's upsetting me.'

She glanced at him briefly and then turned her attention back to the sauce. 'You need to stir that before it sticks. You know, in your own way you're just as easy to read as me. The only difference is that you say the opposite of what you're really thinking. Take now, for example—you say nothing is wrong, but I *know* something is wrong.'

'I really, really don't want to talk about this,' he growled, moving away from her and pacing across the room to the window.

'Because you're afraid that talking will make things worse?' Her voice was soft and she turned off the sauce and walked across to him. 'Have you ever tried talking about it?'

He ignored her question and she nodded.

'I'll take that as a no. You should confide in someone, Ben. It might help.'

A muscle worked in his lean jaw and his broad shoulders were tense. 'Have you finished?'

'For now.' On impulse she stood on tiptoe and kissed his cheek. 'You're a very tough man, Ben, but even tough men are allowed to have feelings. It wouldn't make you less tough to talk about how you feel.'

Without waiting for him to answer, she walked back over to the kitchen area, drained the pasta and divided it between two plates.

'This looks delicious.' She added the sauce and carried the two plates over to the table.

They ate in virtual silence and when they'd finally cleared their plates he glanced across at her, his expression unreadable.

'I didn't know it was possible for you to stay quiet for so long.'

'Well, you've banned so many topics that I don't know what to say any more.'

'You're saying you're lost for words?' A faint smile touched his hard mouth. 'I find that hard to believe, Ellie Harrison.'

She looked at him, encouraged by the reluctant smile in his eyes. Maybe, just maybe—*if she was patient*—she'd eventually persuade him to confide in her.

It was definitely what he needed, she decided.

'Dinner tonight?' Ben lifted his head and his eyes narrowed suspiciously as he looked at Sean. 'I don't know…'

'Please. As a favour to me. Ally's invited a small crowd,' Sean said wearily. 'I need moral support.'

Ben watched him suspiciously. 'Has she invited an available single woman?

'I've no idea. She's invited at least fourteen people so it certainly won't be intimate.' Sean's expression was comical. 'Just what I need mid-week. She says that we all work too hard and never get out so she's bringing a social life to my door. Oh, joy.'

Despite himself, Ben smiled. He'd seen Sean change for the better since he'd married Ally and he knew how much his friend loved his wife.

'All right, I'll come,' he said finally, 'but you can tell Ally from me that if there's any matchmaking I'll wring her neck.'

'I'll wring it for you myself,' Sean promised, picking up a stack of files and rolling his eyes. 'And now I've got to be at a meeting to discuss patient waiting times. If I wasn't upstairs with them wasting time when I could be seeing patients, the waiting time would be considerably shorter, but there we are!'

He strode off down the corridor and then paused as if he'd suddenly remembered something. 'Oh, Ben?'

'What?'

'Can you give Ellie a lift tonight?' Sean clutched the files and didn't quite meet his eyes. 'She's coming, too, and it seems stupid to take two cars when you live next door to each other.'

Ben ground his teeth. Just what he'd been expecting. Except that it hadn't occurred to him that Ellie would be the chosen one. He remembered what she'd said about being in love with him. Was she behind this?

He opened his mouth to tell Sean where to stick his dinner party but his friend had gone without giving him a chance to voice his objections.

He found Ellie in the treatment room, finishing off a dressing. She taped it securely, gave the patient instructions on when to return and then waited for them to leave before turning to him with a smile.

Her smile faltered slightly as she looked at him. 'Ouch—you look angry.'

How was it that she could read him so easily?

Some of his anger dissolved as he registered the concern in her eyes. She certainly didn't look like someone who'd been plotting his future. And, come to think of it, underhand tactics weren't really her style.

'I gather you're going to Sean's tonight.' His voice was harsher than he'd intended and he saw the surprise in her eyes.

'Yes.' She tilted her head to one side and looked at him searchingly. 'Is that why you're angry?'

He gritted his teeth. 'I'm not angry.'

She smiled sympathetically. 'There you go again, saying one thing when you're feeling something quite different. You really must start saying how you feel, Ben. It's very bad for you, denying your emotions all the time.'

He decided to ignore her. 'I'll give you a lift.'

What the hell was he saying? He hadn't even decided whether he wanted to go.

Her face brightened as she tossed the remains of a dressing into the bin and washed her hands. 'You're going, too?'

The surprise in her tone was so genuine that he was left in no doubt that Ellie was innocent of any matchmaking intentions.

Which left Sean.

He was going to kill him.

'It would be great if you could pick me up.' She bustled around the room, clearing up, restocking as she talked, constantly on the go. 'What time?'

'Seven-thirty?'

'Sounds good to me.' She smiled at him. 'I'm really pleased you're going out. Since you arrived here, all you seem to do is work and then go home.'

And that was all he wanted to do.

So why the hell was he picking her up at seven-thirty and taking her out to dinner?

Ellie was in the bathroom, putting the finishing touches to her make-up, when she heard the tap on the door.

'Come in,' she called cheerily. 'Door's open.'

She heard a firm male tread on the carpet and then Ben's voice calling her name angrily.

She flinched.

Oops. Now what?

She took a last glance at her reflection and walked out of the bathroom, bracing herself for a telling-off.

'Don't you ever lock your door?' He was standing in the hallway, broad-shouldered and menacing, his eyes glittering with anger. 'For crying out loud, Ellie, anyone could walk in here!!'

She opened her mouth and closed it again, not sure what

to say. 'Er… "Hello Ellie, you look nice,"' she muttered under her breath, and his jaw tightened.

'I don't care how you look,' he growled. 'I just care that you seem to have no sense of self-preservation whatsoever.'

He didn't care how she looked?

Oh, great.

She gave a wry smile and wrestled with her disappointment. So what was the point of spending the extra time getting ready? All he cared about was whether she locked her door.

'I never lock my door,' she told him, picking up her coat and her bag and blowing Max a kiss. 'For one thing, this is a quiet, civilised area, and for another I live with a big hairy German shepherd who has a tendency to frighten the life out of people.'

He ran a hand over his face and let out a slow breath. 'Ellie, please, promise me that from now on you'll lock your door.'

Why did it bother him so much?

'All right, I'll lock the door. If I remember.' She paused and frowned at him. 'You're very tense. Are you hungry?'

His jaw clenched. 'Ellie, don't start!'

'Maybe a small bacon sandwich?'

He gave a reluctant laugh. 'Has anyone ever told you that you're incorrigible?'

She nodded. 'You. On several occasions. Now, if you're not going to waste time complimenting me on my appearance, and you don't want a sandwich, shall we go?'

He was silent for a moment, his eyes travelling slowly over every inch of her body.

By the time his gaze returned to her eyes her face was flushed and her pulse rate was galloping like a herd of wild horses.

'You look beautiful,' he said finally, and her smile widened.

'Good. I made a special effort.' She walked past him to the door and picked up her keys from the hall table. 'Any time you want to kiss me, feel free.'

'Ellie!' His low growl was a warning but she ignored it and gave him a cheeky grin.

'I just don't want you to worry about my make-up. It's all easily replaceable.'

He gritted his teeth. 'I will *not* be kissing you.'

'Shame.' She stood to one side to let him pass and locked the door behind them. 'In that case, it's going to be a long evening.'

It *was* a long evening.

From the moment they arrived at the Nicholsons' converted barn, it was obvious that he'd been right in his first assessment of the situation.

Sean was trying to pair them off.

Ben gritted his teeth and bit back a sharp comment as Ally ushered Ellie and himself over to an armchair by the flickering log fire.

'We're short of seats so you two will have to share this.' Beaming happily, she handed them drinks and then walked briskly across the room to talk to another couple.

Ben glared after her but then realised Ellie was already sitting on the floor.

'You have the chair,' she suggested, clearly not seeing anything amiss. 'I don't know how much Ally's drunk, but there's no way you and I can both fit into that chair and still be decent.'

Which had been Ally's intention, of course.

If he hadn't been so annoyed, he would have laughed aloud. Despite the elegant dress, Ellie was totally comfortable snuggled up on the rug, her back resting against the chair as she smiled up at him. So much for Ally's elaborate plans.

'Cheers.' She lifted her glass and reached for a bowl of mixed nuts that were on the table. 'Have some of these. They're yummy.'

They talked quietly for about twenty minutes and then Ally called everyone to the table.

'Ellie, you're there, next to Ben.' Ally waved a hand, her eyes gleaming slightly as she seated the rest of her guests and then brought in the starters.

Ellie caught Ally's speculative gaze and spoke to Ben in an undertone.

'What's got into her tonight? She keeps grinning at me.'

'She's trying to pair us up,' Ben said bluntly, and Ellie's eyes widened.

Without speaking, she glanced across the huge room to the armchair, understanding finally dawning.

'Oh.' She chewed her lip and then looked up at him. 'Why?'

Ben shrugged wearily. 'You tell me.'

Ellie was silent for a moment. 'Is this why you were angry earlier?' she asked in a small voice. 'Because you thought I was trying to trap you? You thought I was part of it, didn't you?'

He shifted uncomfortably. That was exactly what he'd thought.

'To begin with, maybe,' he admitted, 'but—'

'Well, that just shows that you don't know me at all, Ben MacAllister,' Ellie said hotly, forgetting to lower her voice. 'I don't play those sorts of games and you of all people should know that. Just because I think I might be in love with you and I *really* want you to kiss me, that doesn't mean I'd go to devious lengths to achieve it!'

There was a sudden silence around the table and Ben

saw the horror on her pretty face as she realised that everyone had heard what she'd said.

'Well, that's good to hear,' he said calmly, ignoring the
curious stares of those around them and brushing her
flushed cheek with the backs of his fingers.

The look she gave him was mortified and she dipped
her head and concentrated on her food, although she didn't
actually eat anything. She just pushed it around her plate
in a state of misery.

Inwardly cursing Ally's lack of tact, he gently felt for
Ellie's hand under the table and gave it a firm squeeze.
She lifted her head and looked at him gratefully.

'I'm really sorry,' she mumbled, pulling her hand away
from his and picking up her bread roll. 'I had no idea.
Truly.'

'I know that.'

'I would never have come if I'd known.'

'It isn't your fault.'

She looked utterly dejected and he felt a strange desire
to drag her into her arms and kiss her until she smiled
again.

Damn Ally and Sean!

'Why is she trying to set you up anyway?'

Ben tucked into his starter. 'Ally thinks that the answer
to everyone's problems is romance.' He noticed that she
still hadn't touched her food.

'And you don't agree?'

Hardly.

'I don't think all problems are so easily solved,' he said
quietly, casting a searching glance in her direction. 'Aren't
you going to eat? You know you get cross if you don't
eat.'

He was rewarded by a gurgle of laughter.

'Isn't that my line?'

'Yes, but I've borrowed it.' He jerked his head towards

her plate. 'Eat, or she'll notice and decide that you're love-sick. We'll never hear the last of it.'

She did as she was told but it felt like a very long eve-ning and he made their excuses as early as he could.

'That was the most embarrassing moment of my life,' Ellie mumbled as she slid into his car. 'I'm never, ever going to talk again.'

There was laughter in Ben's eyes. 'You made their eve-ning. Declaring undying love to me in public must have been more than even Ally hoped for.'

'Don't remind me!' She gave a moan of horror and cov-ered her eyes with her hands. 'You must hate me.'

There was a long silence and when he spoke his voice was soft and there was no trace of laughter in it. 'Ellie, I don't hate you.'

Her hands slipped from her face and she looked at him tentatively. 'You don't?'

'No.'

She looked at him more closely. 'So does that mean you like me?'

'Yes.'

'How much?'

'Ellie!'

'Sorry, sorry.'

Ben started the engine and reversed out of the Nicholsons' drive before indicating right and setting off for home. He drove in silence and when he finally pulled in beside her cabin Ellie plucked up the courage to speak again.

'Would you like to come in?'

She heard his indrawn breath and then he shook his head. 'I don't think that's a good idea.'

She bit her lip. 'Because I'm too young?'

He was silent for a moment. 'That's one of the reasons.'

'I'm nearly twenty-four,' she protested, and he closed his eyes and gave a short laugh.

'Precisely. As I said—too young.'

'You prefer older women?'

He looked at her with exasperation. 'I can't believe I'm having this conversation. Ellie, I don't want any sort of relationship.'

'Well, that's fine by me.' Her cheeks dimpled into a pretty smile. 'But that doesn't mean we can't be friends and have fun, does it?'

He looked at her blankly and she sighed.

'Fun, Mr MacAllister,' she said gently. 'Do you remember what that is? It's when you stop worrying about the future and just enjoy the moment.'

'You don't know what you're saying.' He raked lean fingers through his dark hair and she smiled wistfully.

'Oh, yes, I do.'

'Ellie—' his tone was weary '—I wouldn't be good for you.'

She thought about that for a long moment and then gave a womanly smile. 'I know you'd be good for me and I'm fairly confident that I'd be good for you too,' she said softly, reaching for the door handle and letting herself out. 'So any time you want to put it to the test, let me know.'

CHAPTER SIX

A AND E stayed frantically busy and one afternoon, several weeks after Ben had started, Heather, the A and E receptionist, opened the door to the staffroom and looked round with laughter in her eyes. 'OK, whose turn is it to clean up Freddie Hayward?'

There was a chorus of groans from the staff trying to eat lunch and Ben's eyes narrowed.

'Who is Freddie Hayward?'

'He's a tramp and you can smell him a mile off,' Will Thacker muttered, wrinkling his nose in distaste. 'He was in here last month, just before you started, Ben. It took us hours to clean off the lice and fleas.'

Ellie bit her tongue, knowing full well that Will hadn't gone near Freddie.

'He's clutching his stomach,' Heather said, and Will laughed unsympathetically.

'Too much alcohol. He ought to just go home and sleep it off.'

Ellie stood up quickly. 'Freddie doesn't have a home to go to.' Her voice shaking slightly, she turned to Heather. 'Put him in cubicle one. I'll see to him.'

Nicky frowned. 'Ellie, you didn't take a coffee-break, and you haven't had lunch yet—'

'I'm not hungry.'

Upset by Will's careless attitude, she hurried out of the staffroom, pulled on a plastic apron and a pair of gloves and went to see Freddie.

The A and E department had several regular attendees and Freddie was one of them.

He was sitting hunched in the chair, his clothes stiff with dirt, his eyes closed. His face was whiskery and his hair was shaggy and unkempt. Ellie felt a rush of compassion as she looked at him. It wasn't right that any human being should end up like this.

'Hello, Freddie,' she said gently, her hand on his shoulder as she crouched down to talk to him. 'It's Ellie—remember me?'

Freddie gave a grunt and looked at her through glazed eyes. 'Need to feed the dog.'

Ellie looked at him. 'What dog, Freddie?'

To the best of her knowledge, Freddie didn't have a dog.

'Too old to be left.' He gave a grunt of pain and doubled over. 'Turn first left and we're down the end of the road.'

Ellie stared at him, an uneasy feeling nagging inside her head. 'Freddie, what day is it today?'

'I told them, there's no point in planting them out at this time of year because the frost will get them!' He glared at her and then gave a groan and clutched at his stomach.

'Freddie?' Alarmed, Ellie gave his arm a shake and then put a hand on his forehead. 'Oh, heavens, you're burning up, you poor thing. Let's get this coat off you and put you on the couch so that the doctor can take a look.'

'But will he sell the dog?' Freddie's face crumpled. 'I don't want them to sell the dog.'

'He won't sell the dog,' Ellie said firmly, slipping the filthy coat off Freddie's shoulder and unbuttoning the old cardigan that he wore over a loose-fitting shirt. 'Now, can you climb up on this couch with my help, or do we need some other people?'

Still muttering about frost and dogs, Freddie heaved himself onto the couch and lay down with a groan.

'Can't sleep. Got to report for duty at oh-nine-hundred hours.'

'You've got plenty of time, Freddie,' Ellie soothed as she checked his pulse and popped a thermometer in his mouth.

'I can't be late—' He broke off and cried out in pain, clutching the sides of the trolley, which Ellie had put up to stop him falling off.

'How long have you had this pain, Freddie?' Her voice was urgent but he was lying there clutching his stomach, unable to answer.

Gently she pulled his trousers down, biting her lip when she saw how filthy he was. Poor, poor man. He was badly in need of some attention.

'I'm going to get you some nice clean clothes,' she murmured as she dropped his into a bag to send to the volunteer service. Fortunately they had an army of volunteers who did wonderful things like helping the homeless.

She gently covered him with a blanket and then nipped outside to the corridor in search of a doctor.

The first person she saw was Will, deep in conversation with Ben, and she stopped dead.

She didn't want Will near Freddie.

Ben stopped talking when he saw her. 'Did you want a doctor?'

She nodded warily, avoiding Will's glance. 'I'm worried about Freddie.'

'Why? Has he been taken over by lice?' Will laughed at his own joke and Ellie glared at him.

'You are so insensitive!'

He looked slightly taken aback and immediately defended himself. 'The guy just wants to come in for a bit of free heat and a bath. If we're too nice to him, he'll be here all the time. In case you hadn't noticed, we're too busy to waste our time on no-hopers.' He glanced at his watch. 'Which cubicle is he in? I'll sort him out on my way to lunch for you.'

'That won't be necessary.' Ben's tone was icy cold and he shot the other doctor a contemptuous look before glancing at Ellie with a question in his eyes. 'Where is he?'

She smiled with relief and gratitude. 'I've put him in cubicle one.' As they moved away from Will, she briefed him on what she'd found. 'It may be nothing, but he seems to be in a lot of pain and he's got a temperature and a tachychardia and he's confused.'

He gave a slight smile. 'You have been busy.'

They reached the door of the room and she put a hand on his arm to stop him going in. 'Ben...' She bit her lip and lowered her voice. 'I haven't had time to give him a wash because I was worried there might be something very wrong so I wanted him checked first, but if it bothers you...'

'It doesn't bother me.' He pushed her gently to one side and walked into the room.

'Hello, Mr Hayward.' His tone was warm and respectful and Ellie felt a rush of relief. She should have known that Ben would treat every patient with dignity. 'I'm Dr MacAllister. Ellie tells me you've been having some pains in your stomach. Can you tell me about them?'

'Can't climb to the top in this weather,' Freddie mumbled, and Ben frowned slightly, reaching out a hand for the record card and reading the results of the observations that Ellie had already taken, together with past notes.

'Do you mind if I just feel your tummy?' Very gently Ben examined Freddie's abdomen and the old man howled in pain. Ben's mouth tightened. 'His abdomen is like a board. Fast-bleep the surgical reg and get me a venflon. I need to take some bloods and give him some antibiotics. In my opinion, he could have appendicitis.'

'Do you want me to call Will?'

A slight smile played around Ben's firm mouth. 'I don't think so, do you?'

'Maybe not.' Her heart performed strange antics in her chest as she stared at his mouth, hypnotised by his sexy smile.

He was an incredibly impressive man, she decided. At first glance he seemed tough and unapproachable, but she'd seen how kind he'd been to Lindsay when she'd been desperately afraid, and how warm and respectful he was being now to Freddie who needed medical help so badly. Unlike Will, he clearly didn't make snap judgements based on appearances.

He was the best doctor she'd ever worked with.

And she was crazily in love with him.

'What's wrong?' His searching gaze made her blush and she turned her attention to Freddie, trying hard not to let her feelings show on her face.

She'd suspected it, but now she knew for sure. And she knew that, for her, this was the real thing. She'd never been one to 'fall in love' repeatedly. There'd never been anyone that she'd been interested in as more than a friend.

Until now.

'Ellie?' Ben's tone was slightly sharp. 'I need to take some blood from Freddie.'

She gave a start and pulled herself together.

Blood. From Freddie.

She picked up the right equipment and passed it to Ben with a shaking hand, aware that he was still watching her closely.

After one final, searching look that left her pulse rate in total disorder, he turned his attention back to their patient.

'I need to take some blood from you, Freddie—can I call you Freddie?' Ben was talking calmly, explaining what he was doing as he carried on giving Ellie instructions in an undertone. 'He's shocked, so can you run through some normal saline and then call X-Ray. I want an erect chest X-ray and then I want you to pass a naso-gastric tube…'

He found a vein easily, taped the venflon in place and then injected some antibiotics just as the surgical registrar walked into the room.

Ellie lubricated the end of the tube and eased it gently into Freddie's nose. 'Swallow for me, Freddie,' she urged, and he did as she asked, his eyes suddenly dull and sunken.

Ben briefed the surgical reg and they conferred for a few minutes while Ellie gave Freddie a quick wash and changed him into a hospital gown.

'When they've sorted out your tummy, a nice nurse is going to do your hair,' she told him chattily. 'Full salon treatment. Wash, condition, cut—if you want a cut, that is,' she added quickly, and then broke off as she saw Ben and the registrar exchange amused looks. 'What? What did I say?'

'Nothing.' The registrar gave her a warm smile and she turned her attention back to Freddie, making him as com-fortable as she could in the short time available before he had to have his X-ray.

The registrar picked up the notes and gave them both a nod. 'We'll take it from here. I've rung Theatre and they're expecting him. Have you sent off bloods?'

Ben nodded. 'FBC, U and E, blood sugar and amylase.'

'Great. Thanks.'

'I'll help you with the trolley.' Ellie took Freddie's hand in hers and gave it a squeeze. 'Freddie, you need to have an operation, but when you're better I'll come and visit you and bring you some new clothes.'

'Don't let him shoot the dog,' Freddie mumbled, and the registrar looked startled.

'He's a very nice man. He won't shoot the dog,' Ellie said firmly, making a mental note to speak to the social workers about Freddie. Maybe he did have a dog. It certainly didn't pay to make assumptions.

She wheeled the trolley as far as Theatre and then said her goodbyes, returning to A and E and immediately picking up the phone to Social Services. She spoke to the duty social worker who, it turned out, knew Freddie Hayward very well.

'He was a salesman,' the social worker told her, 'but then he started to drink and lost his job. His wife threw him out and he's been on the streets ever since. He's actually a really nice man. He turns up at the hostel on King Street occasionally. What's happened to him?'

Ellie told her and asked if she knew anything about a dog.

'I've never heard anyone say anything about a dog but I'll ask some questions,' the social worker assured her. 'Which ward will he be on? I'll go and visit him and see if we can sort something out. He won't be able to sleep rough when he's discharged from hospital.'

Feeling thoroughly depressed about Freddie and disconcerted about the strength of her feelings for Ben, Ellie walked back to the treatment room where she'd been put in charge of dressings for the day and started to wade her way through the queue of people.

Her stomach was rumbling but she knew that she couldn't have eaten anything even if she'd had the time, which she didn't.

'That's healing nicely,' she told one lady who'd come back for the second time to have her burn checked. 'You can make an appointment with your practice nurse and they'll carry on dressing it until it's better.'

'Thanks, Nurse.' The lady sat quietly while Ellie carefully dressed the burn. 'It was such a stupid thing to do anyway. Can you believe I knocked the kettle over? And that hot water could do so much damage?'

Remembering the little girl they'd had in, Ellie nodded. 'If you'd just boiled the kettle, then yes.' She fastened the dressing and scribbled on the lady's card. 'Go back to your GP practice for dressings from now on, but if you're worried you can always ring us again.'

The patients kept coming and by four o'clock she was starting to feel light-headed.

She sank into one of chairs and stared into space, jumping out of her skin when the door opened minutes later and Ben walked in.

Her stomach hit the floor and so did the dressing pack she was holding. Tweezers, gauze and gallipots ended up on the ground.

'Oh, help.' Blushing frantically, she stooped to pick them up, making sure that he couldn't see her face.

She knew that she was hopeless at hiding her feelings.

'Are you all right?'

Although she wasn't looking at him, she heard the concern in his tone and she kept her voice bright.

'Yes, fine.'

There was a brief pause and then he gave a sigh. 'Ellie Harrison, you're a hopeless liar. I thought you always said what was on your mind?'

'It's the new me,' she said lightly, retrieving the bits from the dressing pack and putting them back on the trolley. 'I'm going to try and work harder at hiding my feelings.'

She glanced briefly at his black hair and promptly knocked a box of saline off the shelf with her elbow.

Oh, help. Her body was ceasing to function.

'Hiding your feelings?' His tone was amused. 'Ellie, you'd burst if you had to hide your feelings. So are you going to tell me now, or am I going to drag it out of you?'

She fumbled with the box, her cheeks flaming.

Clearly she had to say something.

She tucked a strand of dark hair behind her ear and gave him a brief smile. Then regretted it. Even that quick look had left her feeling scorched. 'I feel really sad about Freddie.' It was the truth. She *did* feel really sad about Freddie. 'What sort of life does he have? He's all on his own...'

Ben leaned broad shoulders against the wall, his eyes never leaving her face. 'You're right. It is sad.'

Ellie was silent for a long moment and then she looked up and managed a smile. 'Well, at least he'll be in the warm and be fed for a few days.'

Ben looked at her steadily. 'Thanks to you. Most people would have taken one look at him and not even considered that something might be wrong.'

She blushed, immensely pleased by the unexpected praise. 'It's dangerous to judge by appearances.'

'Absolutely.' Ben gave her a rare smile, clearly recalling their conversation on the first night they'd met. 'You were very kind to him and very quick to spot the problem. I've spoken to Social Services and they're going to make him a priority.'

'Good.'

There was a long pause. 'So now are you going to tell me what's really wrong? When we were treating Freddie you kept looking at me strangely. And now I walk into a room and suddenly you keep dropping things.' He was frowning at her. 'You may talk too much and do reckless things, but you're not usually clumsy. I think you need to take a break. You've skipped all your breaks again today, which is presumably why you're behaving so oddly.'

'No!' She blurted the denial out before she could stop herself, and he lifted a dark brow.

'No, what?'

'No, I'm not hungry. I couldn't eat a thing.'

'You, not able to eat!' There was laughter in his eyes. 'Ellie, are you ill?'

She stared at him, her breathing shallow. 'No.' There was the briefest of pauses. 'It's just that I'm so in love with you that I'm finding it a bit hard to concentrate.'

The laughter died and the hiss of Ben's indrawn breath was clearly audible.

'I know, I know—you don't want to hear it,' she said hastily, stacking the boxes more neatly on the shelf in the hope that she wouldn't knock anything else onto the floor. 'You needn't worry. I don't expect you to say anything or do anything or feel anything in return. You've made it clear that you don't and that's OK.'

Well, it wasn't OK actually, but what choice did she have?

'Ellie, we've already established that this is a childish crush.'

She shook her head slowly. 'No. You thought that. I wasn't sure. But now I'm sure. I definitely love you.'

There was a long silence and when he finally spoke he sounded tired. 'Ellie, you're very young—'

'So you keep telling me.' She gave him a weak smile. 'But if this is the part where you tell me that this is just a passing infatuation and that I'll get over it, please, don't waste your breath. I don't have passing infatuations. I never have done and I never will do. With me it's all or nothing, and in this case it's definitely "all".'

Ben's shock was palpable. 'You don't know what you're saying.'

'Yes, I do.' She gave a faint smile. 'I suppose I should see the funny side, really. The first time I'm interested in a man, he doesn't know I exist.'

He lifted a hand and rubbed his rough jaw. 'Ellie, believe me, I know you exist.'

She gave a twisted smile. 'But you're not interested.'

She bit her lip. 'Oh, hell, I've never propositioned anyone in my life before and this isn't even a leap year.'

His mouth tightened and he glanced through the glass panel in the doors to the corridor outside, a muscle working in his dark jaw.

'We can't talk about this now,' he said roughly. 'You've got patients waiting.'

'There's nothing to talk about anyway.' She gave him a brave smile. 'I shouldn't have said anything, except that you pushed me and I haven't had as much experience as you at hiding my feelings. Believe me, I'm working on it. In the meantime, please, don't worry about it.'

With a muttered oath he walked to the door and then paused, his hand on the door handle. 'We'll talk about this later.'

Would they?

What was the point? Ben clearly didn't want any sort of relationship with her.

She watched him go and carried on to the end of the shift, her insides in turmoil.

Will caught up with her as she went to get changed to go home.

'Ellie, look, I was an idiot earlier.' He pulled a face. 'I'm sorry.'

'Freddie had appendicitis. Which just goes to show that you were rather judgmental, don't you think?' She looked him straight in the eye and he shifted slightly.

'Absolutely. You're totally right. Ben's already torn a strip off me.'

Ellie stared at him in surprise. 'Oh…'

Well, good for Ben.

'Just to show there are no hard feelings, how about a quick drink after work?'

Ellie hesitated and Will must have sensed a refusal com-

ing because he carried on hastily without allowing her to
speak.

'Everyone's coming. You didn't make the pizza the
other night so why don't you join us?'

She didn't feel like a drink, but she didn't really feel
she could refuse a second time.

'Everyone's going?'

Will examined his fingernails. 'Most people.'

Maybe she'd go for five minutes.

'Just a quick one, then,' she said, and he flashed her a
smile.

'Great. I'll meet you by the door when you're changed.
We can walk over together.'

Ellie stared after him uneasily.

She had one of her feelings...

But what could be wrong with a harmless drink?

Rummaging around for her key, she secured her locker
and made her way through A and E to the staff entrance,
her heart sinking as she saw Ben striding towards her.

'Are you going home?'

She shook her head. 'I'm going for a drink with everyone. I didn't feel I could say no after missing the pizza the
other night.'

He looked at her, his gaze disturbingly direct. 'Who invited you?'

She bit her lip. 'Will Thacker.'

His mouth tightened and she frowned at him, puzzled.

'Are you coming?'

A strange expression crossed his face and he seemed
about to say something but then changed his mind and
shook his head. 'No.'

'Oh.' She tried to hide her disappointment, her heart rate
increasing as he lifted a hand and brushed her cheek with
his knuckles.

'Be careful.'

'I'm only going for a drink.' She shrugged and smiled. 'How dangerous can it be?'

'With you there?' His smile was weary. 'Pretty dangerous. You attract danger like a magnet, Ellie. Stay with your friends and don't talk to strangers.'

How could she have been so naïve?

The minute she and Will arrived at the pub, she realised her mistake. There was no one there from her shift except the two of them.

She turned to him immediately, her tone suspicious. 'Where are the others?'

He didn't meet her eye. 'They'll be along in a minute,' he said casually, walking straight to the bar and ordering them both a drink.

Ellie glanced towards the door, wondering whether he was telling her the truth. Will made her feel uneasy. *He hadn't even asked her what she wanted to drink.*

She stared suspiciously at the glass he handed her and he gave a faint smile.

'It's called alcohol, Ellie, otherwise known as a gin and tonic. Drink it. It will do you good after the day you've had.'

'I don't usually drink alcohol. It makes me fall asleep.' She hesitated and then turned to the barman. 'Can I have a grapefruit juice and tonic mixed together, please?'

She saw Will frown slightly but she didn't care. She hadn't eaten a thing since breakfast. There was no way she'd be able to tolerate alcohol.

'Can we sit down while we wait for the others?'

'Sure.' Will picked up his glass and slipped an arm round her shoulders, guiding her towards a free table.

She and Will had been making small talk for twenty minutes when she realised that there was still no sign of the others.

'Where is everyone?' Her head was decidedly swimmy from lack of food as she stared at him and he lifted her hand to his lips and kissed it.

Instantly she snatched it away, her expression horrified. 'What are you doing?'

'Ellie, Ellie,' he drawled slowly, his lips curling into a smile that made her feel distinctly uneasy. 'Are you really that naïve? I haven't asked anyone else.'

'You haven't?' She stared at him blankly. 'Why not?'

'Because the only person I wanted to spend my evening with was you,' he said smoothly, moving his chair so that he was sitting close to her and sliding a warm hand up her leg. 'I know I upset you earlier and I'm sorry. You're a stunning girl. You must know that I'm interested. Everyone else knows.'

Ellie pushed his hand away and glanced nervously round the bar, reassuring herself that they were in a very public place so he was unlikely to go too far.

'W-Will, that's very flattering,' she stammered, 'but—'

'No buts,' he said hoarsely, his breath warm on her neck as he kissed her. 'I want you, Ellie.'

'No!' She stood up quickly and grabbed her bag. 'I'm really, really sorry Will, but this isn't what I want.'

His face darkened. 'Look, I know I was an idiot earlier, but—'

'This isn't about what happened earlier,' she said hastily, deciding that she'd better put the record straight once and for all. 'I'm not interested in a relationship with you, Will. Not under any circumstances.'

He breathed in deeply and his eyes glittered. 'Ellie, listen, I—'

A harsh male voice interrupted him. 'I think she's probably done enough listening for one night.'

Ellie turned quickly, relief pouring over her as she saw Ben, broad-shouldered and menacing, his feet planted firmly apart as he stood behind them, very much the dominant male.

His usual cool reserve seemed to have been replaced by raw emotion, and for a brief moment she had a glimpse of just how tough Ben MacAllister really was.

'Ben!' Will stumbled to his feet, clearly taken aback to see the consultant standing behind them.

'Ellie told me that you'd invited everyone for a drink tonight,' Ben said with cold derision, 'but clearly you left a few people out. So I invited them for you.'

Will looked towards the door of the bar and his mouth tightened as he saw the rest of the staff of the A and E department trooping in, laughing and chatting.

Ben raised a hand to catch their attention. 'We're over here.'

He waited until they'd all pulled up chairs and ordered drinks and then he closed a hand over Ellie's wrist and spoke to the group in general. 'I hope you don't mind if we make a move. Ellie's not feeling a hundred per cent. It's been a long day.'

There were sympathetic nods all round and Ellie was beyond speech. All she was aware of was the strength of Ben's fingers digging into her wrist.

Without slackening his grip, Ben turned to Will. 'I know you wanted everyone to come for a drink.' He emphasised the word slightly, his tone icy cold. 'So now that everyone is here, I know you won't miss Ellie.'

With that he scooped up Ellie's coat in his free hand and strode out of the room, his strong fingers still clamped around her wrist.

His stride was so long that she virtually had to run to keep up with him.

'Slow down,' she muttered breathlessly as they shot up the stairs and into the alleyway that led to the car park at the front of the hospital. 'Ben, for crying out loud. What's the matter with you? If you're cross with me, just yell at me or something. There's no need to make me run so fast to keep up that I fracture my ankle.'

Still he said nothing, but his grip tightened and she winced slightly at the power of his long fingers.

'Ben—say something,' she pleaded in a small voice, and suddenly he stopped dead and turned to face her.

Faced with such electrifying masculinity, Ellie took a step backwards, dragging breath into her lungs as she stood hypnotised by the expression on his face. He looked every inch the dominant male, all rampant sex appeal and rigidly controlled power.

And then his self-control seemed to snap.

Still not uttering a word, he pushed her back against the wall and kissed her roughly, his long fingers biting into her scalp as he plundered her soft mouth.

Desire exploded inside her and suddenly she was achingly aware of every one of her senses.

She was aware of his hard body pressing her into the wall, of his elusive male scent in her nostrils and the erratic beating of her heart. She felt the erotic slide of his tongue inside her mouth and curled her fingers into the solid muscle of his broad shoulders, determined to feel every part of him.

She tasted the frustration on his hot mouth, felt the urgency in his strong hands as they jerked open her coat. And then he was touching her, his fingers sliding underneath the soft wool of her jumper and finding the softness of her breasts.

Despite the roughness of his mouth and the hardness of his body against hers, his hands were unbelievably gentle as he stroked his fingertips over her hardened nipples through the silky material of her bra. Sensation pierced Ellie's body and she wanted to gasp and cry out, but his mouth was still on hers, capturing the sound.

Heat burned deep within her and instinctively she pushed her hips against him, desperate to feel more of him.

Still kissing her, Ben slid both hands down to her thighs and lifted her so that she straddled him, the hard ridge of his erection pressing against her intimately and raising the heat to such an intolerable level that she knew that if it weren't for their clothes, they would have been making love in this small, dark alleyway.

Aching with frustration, she shifted against him and heard him groan a response as his grip on her thighs tightened.

And then they heard the sound of a door slam and footsteps approaching. He released her immediately, leaving her dizzy and disorientated, her breathing unsteady as she gulped in mouthfuls of the night air.

Ben didn't utter a word. He stood still, arms braced either side of her, every muscle in his body rigid with tension as he fought for control. Then he finally lifted his head and looked at her, his dark gaze burning into the very depths of her soul. It was a look that spoke volumes, a look that left her in no doubt that he wanted her—as if there was any room for doubt after what they'd just shared. She waited for him to speak. To say something about what had just happened between them. But instead he grasped her wrist firmly and propelled her towards the car.

Heart still thumping, she climbed into the passenger seat, wondering what she was supposed to do next.

Was he really going to pretend that it hadn't happened?

That they hadn't just set fire to each other in the small, dark alleyway?

Carefully Ellie turned her head, risking a tentative look at his hard, set profile, but he was firmly back in control of his emotions. It was as if their wild, almost primitive encounter had never happened.

But it had.

She felt as though she'd been caught in the path of a
storm and knew instinctively that her life would never be
the same again.

Where was there to go after that?

Still without speaking, he started the engine and drove
in the direction of home, his eyes firmly fixed on the road
ahead. Finally he pulled up outside her cabin and switched
off the engine.

The silence wrapped itself around them like a cloak.

'Well…' Her voice was croaky in the darkness. 'I was
wrong.'

Ben sat in silence next to her, his body totally still, but
his knuckles white as he clenched the wheel.

'About what?'

'I didn't keep my eyes open.' She nibbled her lip, and
her voice was soft. 'Are you going to kiss me again?'

Finally he turned to face her, his eyes glittering with
anger.

'Just answer me one question. How the hell have you
survived for this long without getting into deep trouble?
You're so damn trusting it's unbelievable—' He broke off
and raked his fingers through his hair, clearly battling with
his temper. 'What made you go with Will? You must have
seen the way he looks at you. Why didn't you get one of
your famous feelings? Couldn't you sense that he was trouble? It was as plain as the nose on your face that there was
something fishy going on. But you just can't see bad in
anyone, can you?'

He stopped, his breathing unsteady, and she gave him a
curious look. She'd never known him talk so much.

Why was he in such a state?

It wasn't as if Will had made a pass at *him*!

She opened her mouth to remind him of the fact but he
raised a hand to stop her speaking.

'Just do me a favour, will you?' His voice was a low

growl and the expression in his dark eyes was stormy. 'Please, try and look for the risk in situations before you throw yourself into them, because one day you're going to get yourself in serious trouble.'

Ellie stared at him in silence for a long moment and felt tears prick her eyes. He obviously thought she was a hare-brained idiot.

'Right.' She gave a weak smile and bent to pick up her bag. 'I'll take that as a no, then.'

'No?' His dark brows met in a frown and she gave a small shrug.

'I take it that means you don't want to kiss me again. It was just a one-off thing. That's fine, no problem.' *Well, big problem actually.* She fumbled with the door handle and slid out of the car, clutching her bag and coat. 'In which case, I'll say good night. Thank you for the lift.'

She walked unsteadily to her cabin, wondering what the kiss had meant to him.

For one, all too brief moment, he'd lost control.

And she knew that he'd wanted her just as much as she wanted him.

But now he was firmly back in control of his emotions again.

What did it take to make Ben let go?

CHAPTER SEVEN

THE atmosphere in A and E was tense the next day.

They were phenomenally busy, short-staffed and tired from working long hours with no breaks.

Will was plainly in a sulk and Ben was silent and moody.

It was a relief to Ellie when Lindsay popped in during the lunch-break to show them the baby.

'She slept for five hours last night without waking up,' Lindsay announced proudly, smiling as they all crowded round to peep at the baby.

'I'm not coming too close in case it's catching,' Sean drawled, winking at Lindsay to take the sting out of his words. 'She's great, Lindsay. Congratulations.'

Ellie took the baby and gave her a cuddle, noticing the sudden tension in Ben's face.

Didn't he like babies?

She handed Storm back to Lindsay, remembering the night he'd delivered the baby. Technically it had been impossible to fault him, but emotionally… She frowned slightly as she cast her mind back to that night. Emotionally he'd kept himself completely detached.

She chatted casually to Lindsay, noticing that Ben stayed only long enough to offer a polite, if reserved greeting.

Did she dare ask him about it?

No.

He'd made it clear enough that he had no intention of opening up to anyone.

Just before the end of Ellie's shift Ambulance Control

rang to warn them that they were bringing in a mother and baby who'd been injured in a car accident.

Sean glanced at Ben, his eyes suddenly wary. 'Perhaps I'd better take this one.'

'No.' Ben's mouth tightened into a grim line. 'I'll take it.'

'But—'

'I'll take it.'

Ben's words were clipped and Ellie glanced between the two men, puzzled. Why were they arguing over who was going to deal with the accident?

Without waiting for further discussion, Ben turned on his heel and strode towards Resus, leaving Ellie and Sean staring after him.

'Damn. I handled that badly.' For once there was no smile on Sean's face. 'Ellie, I want you to watch him for me.'

'I don't understand.' She frowned. 'Why do I need to watch him? He's the best doctor I've ever worked with. What do you think is going to happen?'

What exactly was she watching for?

Sean took a deep breath and there was no mistaking the concern in his face. 'I can't tell you that. I just need you to promise that if you're worried about anything—*anything at all*—you'll come and find me.'

Ellie almost screamed with frustration. She felt totally in the dark. 'Well, of course, but—'

Sean touched her on the shoulder. 'Don't ask me any more. It's time you got to work. You need to get the room ready.'

Still wondering what on earth was going on that she obviously wasn't aware of, Ellie hurried to Resus and pushed open the door.

Ben was standing in the middle of the room, his fingers

gripping the side of the trolley, beads of sweat visible on his brow.

It always happened when he walked into Resus.

Instinctively Ellie stepped towards him. 'Ben…'

He released the trolley and moved away from her, his voice sharp as he issued a string of commands. 'Run through some saline and check the bulb is working in the paediatric laryngoscope. I need a flat blade,' he snapped, and she looked at him in surprise.

In the short time she'd worked with him, she'd hadn't heard him be short with anyone. Yes, he was cool and detached, always the one firmly in control when he gave orders, but he did so calmly and with courtesy.

This was a Ben she didn't know.

Still trying to work out what was happening, she jumped slightly as the doors to Resus crashed open and the paramedics came rushing in, followed by Will.

'She's got no pulse.' The paramedics laid the baby on the trolley and Ben's face paled visibly as he stared down at the tiny form.

The paramedic carried on briefing him. 'The mother was driving too fast and hadn't fastened the seat belt properly. The little one hit the seat in front.'

A muscle worked in Ben's jaw and he didn't move. It was as if he was frozen to the spot.

Ellie licked her lips, her eyes on his face. 'Will, bleep the paediatricians, please. Ben, do you want to intubate her?'

He didn't respond, his eyes still on the baby, and then suddenly, just when she was thinking that maybe she'd better call Sean, he seemed to pull himself together.

'Will, get a line in while I intubate her. Ellie, she needs to be attached to a monitor. Get some leads on her now and someone fast-bleep the paediatricians.' Ben barked out a string of instructions, all his attention focused on the baby. 'Give me a straight-blade laryngoscope and an un-cuffed ET tube.'

Breathing a sigh of relief, Ellie slapped a tiny laryngo-scope into his hand and adjusted the light so that he could visualise the baby's vocal cords.

'OK…' Without lifting his gaze from the tiny airway, he snapped his fingers impatiently and she gave him the tiniest ET tube, which he carefully eased down the baby's trachea. 'That's good.'

He carefully removed the metal laryngoscope and Ellie took it from him while he ventilated the baby with oxygen.

Satisfied that the baby was now intubated, Ellie quickly set about sticking leads on the baby's chest so that they could monitor the heart rate.

They all looked at the monitor and Ben's mouth tight-ened.

'She's in EMD,' he muttered. 'Something is obstructing her output.'

EMD—electromechanical dissociation—meant that al-though a patient's ECG showed electrical activity in the heart, there was no pulse.

Ellie bit her lip and felt the tension building inside her as she looked at the tiny body on the trolley.

Surely Ben could save her?

She almost laughed at her own thoughts. Being in love was making her blind to the facts. Ben might be one hell of a good doctor, but the baby was extremely badly in-jured.

Will was desperately trying to find a vein. 'This is hope-less.'

Ben was examining the baby again, his face set and determined as he searched for a cause. 'She's got tracheal deviation,' he said, straightening up and glancing round the assembled team. 'This baby has a tension pneumotho-rax. Will, have you got a line in yet?'

His voice was sharp and sweat beaded on Will's brow. 'No. It's impossible.' There was no trace of his usual flippancy. 'Everything seems to have shut down. There's nothing.'

Ben's expression was grim. 'Let me try. You take over here.'

The two doctors swapped places and Ben picked up the baby's tiny hand, flicking it gently with his finger to try and find a vein.

'See what I mean?' Will's tone was quiet. 'Nothing. We'll have to use an intraosseous needle.'

In small children an infusion was sometimes given straight into the bone if a vein couldn't be located quickly.

Ben ignored him, all his attention focused on the tiny hand in front of him. Eyes slightly narrowed, he rubbed the skin again and then glanced briefly at Ellie.

'Squeeze here for me.'

She did as he'd instructed and he took the tiny venflon and slid it under the skin. Blood flowed backwards and there was a collective sigh of relief.

'My God, you've done it!' Will stared in amazement and then gave a short laugh. 'Have you got X-ray eyes?'

Ben didn't respond. He was too busy trying to save the baby's life. His hands as steady as a rock, he strapped the venflon firmly in place and glanced up at the ECG monitor. 'Get me some normal saline, and give her a bolus of 20 mils. I suspect she's hypovolaemic. We need to sort out this pneumothorax. Where the hell are the paediatricians?'

'Right here.' The consultant strode up to the trolley and Ben handed him the cannula.

'That's what I call immaculate timing. I'll leave this job to you if you don't mind.'

His colleague gave a brief nod and inserted the cannula into the lower part of the intercostal space. As he withdrew the needle there was a hiss of gas.

'Any sign of a pulse?'

Ellie taped the cannula to the chest wall and the paediatrician gave a nod to his team. 'We need to put in a chest drain and take an X-ray.'

'She's got a pulse!'

Ben's face cleared and he closed his eyes briefly. 'Thank God. All right, we need to check her for other injuries. Let's get her stable and then you chaps can take her.'

The paediatrician was still working on the baby. 'Has anyone spoken to the parents? What happened?'

Ben's mouth tightened and something flickered behind his dark eyes. An emotion that Ellie couldn't interpret. When he spoke, his voice was businesslike.

'Apparently the mother was driving too fast and hadn't fastened the little one's seat belt properly. She was in the back.'

'So she must have hit the front seat...' The other doctor gave a slow nod as his mind raced through other possible injuries. 'So that's where the pneumothorax came from, then. Let's see what else is lurking.'

It was another hour before the baby was stable enough to be transferred to the paediatric intensive care unit.

'Ellie, can you find the mother and tell her that I'll be with her in five minutes?' Ben's expression was suddenly strained and Ellie frowned.

'Why don't you go and grab a cup of tea or something?' she suggested quietly. 'I'll deal with the mother until you're ready to talk to her.'

'No.' He shook his head and took a deep breath. 'I just need a minute, alone.'

'Ben—'

'Alone!'

His voice was a growl and she swallowed and backed away, hating to leave him but helpless to know what else to do.

He clearly wasn't prepared to open up to her, to tell her what was wrong, and instinctively she knew that it would be wrong to press the issue. This wasn't the time or the place.

But later on, when they were home...

She pushed open the door of the relatives' room and frowned as she saw the slumped figure of a woman in one of the chairs.

'Mrs Williams? Tina?' Ellie's voice was gentle as she walked quietly across the room and crouched down beside her. 'Has anyone been in to see you?'

The woman sniffed and nodded, her eyes swollen with crying. 'The doctor said that she almost died. And it's all my fault.' Her face crumpled again and Ellie slipped an arm around her.

'She's been taken up to Intensive Care but so far she seems to be doing all right.'

'I never should have driven so fast,' the woman whispered, 'but I panicked.'

Ellie frowned. 'Why did you panic?'

The woman swallowed and shredded a tissue. 'Because of *him*.'

'Him?' Ellie took a wild guess. 'Your husband?'

'Ken Foggarty is not my husband.' Tina Williams gave a sob. 'I'll never be able to marry him now. And I told him so. And that's why he did it. He was furious with me.'

Ellie was struggling to make sense of what she was saying. 'What did he do?'

The woman took a shuddering breath and shook her head. 'I can't tell you.'

'But—' Ellie broke off as the door opened and Ben walked in, his handsome features strained and tense.

'Mrs Williams?' His tone was unusually short and Ellie frowned slightly as Ben described the baby's injuries and what had been done so far.

He was cool and unemotional, with none of the empathy she'd seen him show to patients before.

'I should never have driven so fast,' the woman whispered again, and Ben's face was expressionless.

'So why did you?'

'Ben…' Ellie tried to catch his eye, aware that he'd misunderstood the situation and not wanting him to make things worse. But far from being offended by his curt question, Tina seemed to take it as a cue to blurt out the whole story.

'Because he was after us,' she sobbed, huddling her arms round her waist as if for protection. 'I told him that I wouldn't marry him and he just lost it. He was throwing things. He—he said he hated Fiona—said it was all her fault.'

Ellie handed her another tissue. 'How could it be a baby's fault?'

Tina gave a twisted smile. 'Irrational, isn't it? But, then, that's Ken all over. He blames Fiona for the fact that things have gone wrong between us. He reckons that before she came along we were happy, and maybe we were.' She sniffed and rubbed her eyes with the back of her hand. 'But once the baby was born, he changed.'

'In what way?' Ellie prompted her gently, aware that Ben was standing as still as a statue in the far corner of the room, his face a mask.

'It was like he resented every moment I spent with her.' She blew her nose. 'He was…angry all the time.'

'Did he hurt you physically?'

Tina nodded. 'Every time I paid the baby any attention.'

'And did he hurt Fiona?'

'Not so far, but I suppose it's only a matter of time. Every time she cries he boils up inside, and she's teething at the moment so…' She broke off and looked at Ellie helplessly.

'I can imagine.' Ellie gave her shoulder a squeeze. 'So what happened today to make you leave?'

The woman swallowed. 'I told him once and for all that I wasn't going to marry him and he went berserk. I managed to lock him in the house and I made a dash for the car, but he was only seconds behind me. That must be why I didn't do her seat belt up properly.' She started to sob again. 'I was so desperate to get away from him that my hands were shaking.'

'And that's why you drove too fast,' Ellie finished for her, shooting a glance at Ben, checking that he'd understood the situation. 'Tina, you know that you need to get the police involved, don't you?'

She gave a sniff. 'The crazy thing is that I really didn't want to. I know he isn't perfect, and you'll think I'm crazy, but I still love him. I really, really love him. But I've got no choice about involving the police. They're already involved. I shot two red lights and caused an accident.'

'Well, you need to involve them in the other part of your life, too,' Ellie urged. 'You must tell them about Ken. Tell them everything you've told us. For Fiona's sake, if not your own.'

There was a long silence and the woman nodded. 'Yes. You're right, of course. I just don't see how they can help.'

'It's worth a try,' Ellie said stoutly. 'At least they can talk to him about the violence. He can't do that to you, Tina.'

Tina looked at her pityingly. 'You don't know Ken. He isn't afraid of the police. They won't be able to stop him. Our only hope is to get away from him completely, give him some time to think things through. That's what I was planning to do before we crashed.' She started to sob again. 'And now she's here and he'll find us. They'll never be able to protect us from him.'

Ellie looked at Ben but his expression was unreadable.

'The police are waiting to talk to you now,' he said quietly. 'I suggest you see them before you go upstairs to visit your daughter.'

Tina sniffed and nodded slowly. 'You're right. It's time I told them the truth.'

'I'll go and find them.'

Ben left the room and by the time Ellie had made Tina a cup of tea and had left her spilling all to the policemen, there was no sign of him.

Where had he gone?

She found Sean in his office. 'Have you seen Ben?'

'Has he vanished?' Sean's expression was grim. 'Well, I suppose that was inevitable in the circumstances.'

'What circumstances?' Ellie looked at him in confusion. 'Why is it inevitable that he's vanished? What on earth is going on, Sean?'

There was a long silence and then Sean gave a long sigh. 'It's not my place to tell you, angel. You'll have to ask him.'

'I have,' Ellie said softly. 'Repeatedly. But he won't open up to me.'

Sean's broad shoulders sagged slightly, as if she'd given him bad news. 'Then there's nothing more that can be done.'

Oh, wasn't there?

Ellie lifted her chin. 'We're not that busy at the moment,' she said in a small voice. 'Maybe if I could slip off a bit early...'

Sean looked her straight in the eye. 'Go. I'll square it with Nicky. Oh, and, Ellie...' His voice stopped her as she reached the door. 'Don't be surprised if he doesn't let you in.'

Ellie gave a slight smile. She wasn't going to rely on Ben to let her in. She had a key.

*　　*　　*

Ben's cabin was in darkness.

Ellie pulled up outside, switched off the engine and stared at the windows. Not a single flicker of light.

Was he there?

He'd had a stressful day. Maybe he was asleep.

But all her instincts told her that there was no way Ben was going to be sleeping tonight. She sensed that whatever it was that was torturing him was too acute to allow him the easy release of sleep.

The sensible thing would be to go straight to her own cabin and leave him in peace. But there was no way she'd be able to sleep herself until she was satisfied that he was all right.

She had this feeling...

Taking a deep breath, she climbed out of the car, walked over to the cabin and tried the door.

It wasn't locked and she opened it gingerly, still not entirely sure she was doing the right thing.

She tiptoed into the cabin and saw him immediately. He was sitting in total darkness, his long legs stretched out in front of him as he stared out of the window across the lake.

He sat totally immobile, as if he'd been there for a lifetime and had forgotten how to move. Even without seeing his face she sensed the depth of his suffering.

Had he even heard her enter the cabin?

If he had, then he gave no sign of it.

'Ben?' She moved slowly so that she was standing in front of him, whispering his name gently. It struck her that it was odd to whisper when there were only the two of them in the cabin, but something about the way he sat— his unnatural stillness—made her afraid to disturb him.

Tentatively she looked down at him, afraid of what she might see but totally unprepared for the raw pain that was clearly reflected in those dark eyes when he finally turned his head to look at her, his expression illuminated by the evening light outside.

Ellie ceased to breathe, stunned into silence by the depth of his anguish. What terrible secret was locked inside him? What was it that hurt so badly that he felt couldn't share it?

Driven by a need to comfort him, she sat down next to him on the sofa, bracing herself for rejection.

What should she say?

What could a person possibly say when confronted by such desolation?

If he didn't want to talk—if he couldn't talk—then that was fine by her, but she needed him to know that he wasn't alone so she did the thing that seemed most natural.

She put her arms around him.

'I love you, Ben.'

She spoke the words softly, and for several heartbeats she held her breath, wondering whether he'd even heard her.

And then he gave a low groan and slid his fingers into her dark hair, lifting her face to his. For endless seconds he stared down at her, clearly fighting his own emotions until finally he seemed to lose the inner battle he'd been fighting and bent his head and took her mouth.

His kiss was rough and hot and it swept her away with the force of a hurricane. It was the kiss of a man who was seeking oblivion. An escape from whatever pain held him so tightly in its grasp. Maybe that should have bothered her, but it didn't.

She loved him.

She was willing to be his comfort, even if it was only temporary.

She was willing to be anything he wanted her to be.

His mouth ravaged hers with a savage urgency and she

gasped as shafts of hot, stabbing pleasure exploded inside her body. She felt his hands move to the neck of her soft, wool cardigan and then the tiny buttons were flying onto the floor as he ripped it impatiently apart, exposing the flimsy lace bra.

His mouth left hers and he trailed hot kisses down her neck to the swell of her breasts which lifted and fell under her rapid breathing.

Her whole body was quivering and the first touch of his mouth on her hardened nipple made her cry out in frustration. She arched beneath him, her whole body liquid with desire, and he unfastened her bra with one flick of his skilled fingers. The sensations threatened to drive her wild.

Desperate for more, she clutched at the hard muscles of his shoulders and then she felt his hands on her jeans, dispensing with the zip in one easy movement and jerking the fabric down her smooth thighs.

In her state of heightened excitement she could barely breathe. All she could do was feel. The pounding of her heart. The firm touch of his long fingers as he tore her flimsy pants in his desperation to remove her clothes and have her naked beneath him.

She'd never been in this position before. Maybe she should have been nervous or shy, but he was moving so quickly that she had no time to feel either. She felt the hard ridge of his arousal pressed against her and knew that they were both well beyond the point of turning back.

And he still hadn't said a word.

Without speaking, he found what he'd been searching for and she gasped as she felt his fingers touching her intimately, exploring and teasing her until she sobbed against his hot mouth.

Whimpering with frustration, she fumbled frantically with his zip, almost crying with relief when his hand covered hers and he helped her complete the task.

Feeling bold in the semi-darkness, she tugged down his trousers and freed him, her mouth drying as she touched him for the first time.

She felt a brief flash of trepidation but already he was above her, leaving her no time for doubts or fears as he thrust hard into her waiting warmth.

Her eyes flew wide as she felt him slide full length inside her and she cried out in ecstasy, her fingers clutching at his shoulders.

Still Ben didn't speak, neither did he slow the pace, taking her hard and fast until she was crying out with pleasure, instinctively moving her hips to match the rhythm he set. It was wild and primitive and Ellie responded to his savage urgency with a desperation that matched his driving need, the feeling inside her so intense that if she hadn't loved him and trusted him, *if it hadn't been Ben holding her*, she would have been terrified.

But it *was* Ben and she clung to him tightly, knowing that wherever the passion took her he would be there, too.

The intense pleasure built to an intolerable level and she was aware only of the solid weight of him on top of her, the powerful thrust of his body inside her as he quickened and deepened his movements.

And suddenly, like a breathless ride on a roller-coaster, it was over, their bodies exploding together in a feeling so agonisingly perfect that it left her breathless and sobbing and clinging to him.

For a long moment he didn't move, and then finally, very slowly, he rolled onto his back, taking her with him, cradling her head against the softness of his shirt as they lay in the darkness.

But still he didn't speak and neither did she.

Her body had expressed her feelings more eloquently than words could have.

What was there left to say?

CHAPTER EIGHT

WHEN Ellie awoke, she was alone.

Still groggy from sleep, she yawned and sat upright, glancing round the cabin for signs of Ben.

But the cabin was empty. In fact, it looked as though she'd been the only inhabitant for some time.

The only sign of their explosive night together was her clothes, piled neatly on the chair opposite.

She stared at the soft duvet tucked around her and wondered when he'd covered her up. It hadn't been while she'd been awake, or she would have remembered.

So where was he?

And why had he left? Was it a sign that he regretted what had happened between them?

Soft colour touched her cheeks as she remembered how she'd behaved. He might have been the one to start it, but she'd been with him all the way.

She nibbled her lip anxiously. *Had she shocked him?*

She'd certainly shocked herself.

She'd had no idea that she was capable of such powerful emotions.

Even if he did regret it, how could she? It had been the most special night of her whole life and she'd do it again in a moment.

Except that he didn't seem to be in agreement.

Accepting that he wasn't coming back, she slid off the sofa and retrieved her clothes, glancing out of the window at the weak, winter sunlight.

Ben was standing by the lake, his back towards her, and

her legs turned to cotton wool as her eyes hungrily scanned his broad shoulders and long, strong legs.

She dressed quickly, dragged on a fleece and hurried outside to find him, her feet making a soft crunching sound as she tiptoed over the frozen grass.

He must have heard her approach but he didn't turn. Instead, she saw a barely imperceptible stiffening of his shoulders as he sensed her presence.

She gave a shiver and huddled deep inside her fleece. 'It's too cold out here,' she said quietly. 'You should come back inside.'

For a moment she thought he wasn't going to answer her, and then he turned, his expression blank as he looked down at her. Ellie's heart sank.

He regretted it.

Well, she wasn't going to worry about that now.

'Ben, please, come back inside.' She touched his arm gently and he shook his head.

Finally he spoke, and his voice had an early morning roughness about it. 'I owe you an apology.'

'For what?'

'Do you really need to ask that?' He raked a lean hand through his dark hair, his gaze incredulous. 'After what I did last night?'

'What *we* did, Ben. I was there, too, remember. And there's certainly nothing to apologise for.'

'How can you be so relaxed about it?' He stared into her eyes for a long moment, his jaw tightening. 'Or do you do this sort of thing all the time?'

He had to be kidding!

She gave a lopsided smile. 'Never in my life before.'

Some of the tension left his shoulders. 'You've never had a one-night stand before?'

She hesitated and then decided to tell him the truth. 'I've never had sex before.'

The silence was so loud it screamed at her.

When Ben finally spoke his voice was hoarse. 'You've never had sex before? You're telling me that was your first time?'

'Yes.'

What was the point of lying? She loved him and she wasn't ashamed of what they'd done.

'Oh, Ellie…' He gave a groan and rubbed a hand over his roughened jaw, his dark eyes haunted. 'Why the hell didn't you tell me? Why didn't you try and stop me?'

'Because I didn't want to stop you,' she said simply. 'Why would I have tried to stop you?'

'Because it wasn't how your first experience should have been.' He sounded weary. 'You should have been with someone who took more time, who paid you more attention…'

'Ben, I was as desperate as you were,' she pointed out, and the shyness which had failed to surface the night before suddenly appeared and she pulled a face. 'This is becoming embarrassing, isn't it? Can we just drop the subject?'

'I don't think we can.' His voice was heavy. 'Ellie, we have to talk about this.'

'Why? What is there to talk about?'

'Are you seriously telling me that you're happy for your first time to be a one-night stand?'

Was that all it had been?

She winced slightly at the brutality of his words but refused to look away from him.

'Obviously I'd like a lot more than that. But whatever you want is fine by me.' She paused. 'I love you Ben.'

His mouth tightened. 'I wish you'd stop saying that.'

'Why? It's true. I do love you. I can't change that. It's not as if I expect you to say it back.'

He closed his eyes briefly. 'Ellie, you're very young and

I'm the first man you've ever slept with. It's normal to have confused feelings.'

'My feelings aren't confused. They're very clear,' she said firmly. 'And I knew that I loved you before we spent the night together.'

His jaw clenched. 'Why? Why did you come to my cabin last night?'

'Because I was worried about you.' She stepped closer to him and tucked a strand of hair behind her ear. 'I thought you might need someone. And you did.'

He stared down at her and for a brief moment she thought he was going to drag her into his arms again, but then he moved away from her and turned towards the lake so she could no longer see his expression.

'I did need someone—' his voice was harsh '—but I wish it hadn't been you. Especially after what you've just told me.'

'Why?'

'Because now you're going to expect something I'm not in a position to give.' He turned to face her, his eyes devoid of expression. 'I can't be in a relationship with you, Ellie. And if that hurts you, I'm sorry.'

The wall was back. The impenetrable defence that he put between himself and the outside world.

'What hurts me is that you won't confide in anyone,' she said quietly. 'It isn't good to bottle things up. And don't pretend that there's nothing wrong. I may be young, but I'm not blind or stupid. I see what happens to you every time you go near Resus. You should talk about it, Ben. It might help.'

There was a long silence while he stared at her, and then his mouth tightened. 'All right,' he said finally. 'After last night I owe you an explanation. At least then you'll understand why this thing between us would never work.'

Ellie shivered slightly, not just because of the freezing

air, but also because of his icy tone and the bleak expression in his eyes. He was only wearing a shirt and she desperately wanted to suggest that they go inside, but she was afraid that he might change his mind about talking to her.

'My wife was very young when I met her. Just seventeen.'

Ellie flinched slightly. *Dear God, it hadn't occurred to her that he might be married.*

Hiding her disquiet, she prompted him gently. 'Go on.'

'I was twenty-three, just finishing med school. I wasn't keen to get married too quickly, I wanted her to go to university and have a life, but she insisted that she loved me and wanted to marry me.' His laugh was bitter. 'In fact, what she loved was the fact that I was almost a doctor. It sounds glamorous when you're a teenager.'

Ellie stared at him. 'So you married her?'

'Yes, on her eighteenth birthday.'

'And then what happened?'

He shrugged. 'We were happy enough, or at least I thought we were. I knew that she resented the long hours I worked, but I thought she knew what she was taking on before she married me. Being married to a doctor is never easy. She was young, she wanted a social life, and I tried to take her out as much as I could.'

Knowing just how hard most doctors worked, particularly in the first years of their career, Ellie thought it sounded exhausting.

'And?'

'And eventually we had a baby.'

A baby...

Something in his tone sent a cold tingle down her spine.

This was going to be bad.

She had one of her feelings.

'Don't tell me, she felt trapped because she couldn't go out?'

He stared into the blackness of the lake, lost in thought, and then finally stirred, drawing in breath and giving a short laugh. 'Oh, she went out.'

Ellie stayed still, waiting for him to tell her the rest. He wasn't looking at her now, all his attention focused on the lake, but she knew that he hadn't finished the story.

'She'd wait for me to come home from work, fling our daughter at me and then go off to a party until the early hours.'

'Oh, Ben...'

'The sad thing is, her partying didn't really bother me.' His tone was almost conversational as he related the tale. 'By then we both knew that we'd made a mistake. She suddenly discovered that there was a whole life out there that she'd missed by being with me from such a young age. I discovered that I needed more in a partner than a pretty face. I didn't mind her going out, and I was more than happy to care for Hannah. I even rationalised it to myself. She'd been in all day with the baby so she had a right to go out in the evenings.'

'So you were staying together because of Hannah?'

'I suppose so.' He gave a brief shrug. 'Plenty of couples do that. And then one day she called me to say that she wanted to go out that evening and needed me to be home. I promised to do my best, but we had a major pile-up to deal with and I was delayed in A and E.'

'Go on.' Ellie's voice was barely a whisper as she prompted him, afraid of what she was going to hear.

He straightened and breathed out heavily. 'I was just about ready to leave when the ambulance arrived with more RTA victims. This time it was my wife and daughter.'

'Oh, Ben...' She covered her mouth with her hand and

tried to resist the temptation to put her arms around him. It was clear from his body language that he didn't want to be touched.

'She'd grown tired of waiting for me so she went to the party anyway and took Hannah with her. Only she didn't fasten the straps of her car seat properly and she didn't bother with her own seat belt at all.' His face was a mask, not a single emotion showing as he related the tale. 'My wife was killed instantly and my daughter died of severe injuries in Resus and I couldn't do a damn thing to save her.'

His face was blank of emotion and she felt tears lodge her throat, threatening to choke her.

'Oh, no…' Unable to contain herself any longer, she slipped her arms around him, ignoring the fact that he didn't respond.

No wonder he'd left A and E for two years. No wonder he couldn't bear to be in Resus. The memories must be horrendous. Too much for anyone to bear.

'So now you know.'

'Does anyone else know?'

'Sean and Ally. That's why they're always trying to interfere with my life. They think that a new relationship can take the pain away. They're wrong.'

Ellie reached up and stroked his face gently. 'Why didn't you tell me sooner?'

'What difference would it have made?'

'Doesn't it help to talk?'

'Nothing helps,' he said shortly. 'Time is supposed to heal, but it doesn't seem to have done a very good job in my case. I suppose that's the guilt.'

'Guilt?' She looked at him in astonishment. 'What do you mean, guilt?'

'I should never have married her, or left her on her own.' Ben pulled away and paced towards the lake, kicking a stone onto the frozen surface and watching as it slid away from them. 'She wanted an exciting life, and I was working too hard to give her what she needed.'

'But that wasn't your fault, Ben.'

'I had reservations about her age and lack of experience when I married her,' he pointed out grimly. 'It turned out that I was right.'

'But the way she was, the way she behaved, had nothing to do with age,' Ellie reasoned. 'It was her personality. And that was her responsibility, not yours. It was she who let Hannah down, not you.'

There was a long pause and then he turned to face her, his eyes haunted. 'Every time I walk into Resus I see her little body. *I couldn't save her.*'

'You're the best doctor I've ever worked with. If you couldn't save her then no one could have saved her,' Ellie said softly, 'and that's the most dreadful, sad thing to have to live with. But it doesn't make the blame yours. Think of all the people that you *have* saved over the years, like that little girl last night. Because of you, she's alive. You've made a difference to so many people's lives.'

His fists were clenched by his sides. 'But not my daughter's.'

'You're a brilliant doctor, Ben. Probably the best I've ever worked with.' Her voice trembled with sincerity as she spoke. '*But you're not God.* You can't perform miracles. If she was that badly injured, no one could have saved her.'

'I let her down.'

'No.' Ellie's eyes were brimming with tears. 'You were the very best father. How can you doubt that?'

Some of the bleakness left his eyes and he cupped her face in his hands and stared down at her.

'You're a nice person, Ellie Harrison, do you know that?

You deserve to meet a fantastic man who'll make you happy.'

She was choking on her tears. 'I've already done that.'

He shook his head and released her immediately. 'Don't say that, Ellie. After everything I've told you, surely you can see how impossible it is.'

'Because of my age?'

'Not just that. Also your total lack of experience. Sooner or later you'll decide you want more.'

'Ben, I'm not like your wife. I like to party sometimes, but I'm equally happy curled up at home or walking in the hills. And I might not have slept with anyone before last night, but that was through choice. It never felt right before.'

'And last night felt right?'

'Oh, yes.' Her eyes were misty. 'Totally right.'

Ben looked at her in disbelief. 'Ellie, I ripped your clothes off and made love to you without any preliminaries at all. It was wild and primitive and I was very rough with you. It was hardly the way you must have imagined your first time would be.'

'No, it was miles more exciting,' she whispered, and he groaned and ran a hand over his face.

'Don't do this to me, Ellie. It won't work.'

She stood on tiptoe and kissed his rough cheek. 'It would work. If you'd only learn to show your feelings instead of keeping them locked up inside. Just remember that I love you, and I'm always here for you. I won't ever change my mind. And if it takes you ten years to decide that you want to be with me, I'll still be here.'

And with that she turned on her heel and walked quickly back to the cabin, leaving him with his thoughts.

Ben stared at the X-ray without seeing it. Instead he saw Ellie's wide-eyed, trusting expression as he thrust into her and sought oblivion.

He'd used her to escape from the agony that pursued him, and for a brief moment he'd succeeded.

But in trying to wipe out one problem, he'd created another.

He closed his eyes briefly and breathed in deeply.

What had he done?

For the first time in his life his rigid code of self-discipline had let him down. He'd acted purely for selfish reasons, using wild, out-of-control sex to drive tortured thoughts from his head.

And now he had to face the consequences.

Ellie wanted more, and he couldn't give her more.

He wasn't prepared to take that risk.

'Er—Ben? Dr MacAllister?'

He suddenly remembered Will standing next to him. 'Sorry—what did you say?'

Will cleared his throat. 'I thought there was a fracture of the ulna but the radius seems OK.'

Ben blinked and focused again on the X-ray. 'What's the history?'

'She slipped on the ice and fell onto her outstretched hand.'

Ben nodded. 'It's rare to fracture one bone in isolation,' he told the other doctor as he stared at the X-ray again. 'Look for a second dislocation injury. In this case, she's dislocated the radial head.'

Will looked again. 'But—' He broke off and his face cleared as he stared at the X-ray. 'Yes, you're right. I do see it now.'

'It's called a Monteggia fracture.' Ben glanced over his shoulder, wondering what time Ellie would arrive.

How were they going to work together?

'Listen, Ben.' Will rubbed a hand along the back of his neck, clearly embarrassed. 'About the other night, in the bar.'

It was a subject that they hadn't touched on since, and Ben felt something hot start to burn inside him. Just thinking about Will with Ellie made his temper rise.

'Let's just forget it,' he said coldly, 'but try and remember that when a girl says no, she means no.'

And if Will Thacker ever laid a finger on Ellie again...

Ben clenched his fists as he wrestled with feelings of jealousy that were totally new to him.

What on earth was the matter with him?

One minute he was telling her to find someone else, but the mere thought of her with someone else drove him mad.

He needed to get on with some work before he lost his grip on reality. Fortunately, at that moment Nicky popped her head into the cubicle to tell him that Mrs Williams was waiting in the corridor and wanted to talk to him.

Wondering what had happened, he gave Will a curt nod and strode out of the cubicle to find Fiona's mother.

She was hovering self-consciously in the corridor and she hurried towards him as she saw him approach. 'Oh, I was hoping that you weren't too busy to see me.'

He saw the tears brimming in her eyes and frowned sharply. 'Is something wrong? Is Fiona worse?'

'No.' She shook her head. 'She's doing very well, thanks to you.'

Ben felt relief flood through his veins. 'I'm glad she's all right.'

'She wouldn't be if you weren't such a clever doctor,' Tina said, her voice choked. 'I was in such a panic yesterday I didn't have time to thank you properly, but the staff on ITU have done nothing but marvel at the fact that you managed to save her. I just can't imagine what it must be like to be so clever that you can save people from death.'

Ben frowned. 'Mrs Williams—'

'Don't say anything.' She held up a hand and sniffed. 'I know you're going to say it's just a job, but the thing is that it's so much more than that to me. You saved my baby's life and there are no words to express how I feel about that. What's it like, going to bed at night knowing that you've kept a family together?'

Ben cleared his throat. 'Well, I can't honestly—'

'That's all I came to say,' she interrupted him quickly, blowing her nose hard and scrunching up the tissue. 'Just thanks. Such an inadequate word for everything you've done, but I don't know any other way to put it.'

With that, clearly embarrassed by the whole encounter, she hurried back down the corridor, leaving him staring after her.

For a moment he didn't move.

Saving the child had been automatic, a response to years of training. He'd never really stopped to think about the impact of those skills on the relatives. But Mrs Williams was right. He'd managed to spare her the agony that he'd experienced.

But he knew that it could easily have gone the other way. Yes, he'd used his skills, but he'd been lucky, too. Fiona's injuries hadn't been as severe as his daughter's had been.

So why did he lie awake at night, blaming himself for not being able to save her?

He was staring into space, thinking logically for the first time in two years, when Nicky tugged at his arm.

'Earth to Ben—I need a doctor in Resus. Ambulance Control have just called. They're bringing in a man who's fallen off a three-storey building. He was working on a building site and a platform collapsed. He's conscious but with a severe leg injury. Oh, and by the way...' She frowned as she remembered something else. 'The police have been trying to find Ken Foggarty, Fiona's father. Apparently he's gone missing and they're worried that he might turn up here. They've asked us to call them immediately if anyone spots him. And we're not to approach him because he might be violent.'

Ben opened his mouth to reply but they heard the sounds of the ambulance approaching so he just nodded briefly and went to meet the paramedics as they hurried in with the stretcher.

'Straight into Resus,' Ben ordered, and the paramedics briefed him as they hurried through the swing doors.

'This is Mike Richards, aged 34. Fell three floors onto wooden planks. He's got a compound fracture of his shaft of femur but no other visible injuries apart from a few bruises. GCS of fourteen.'

'All right, let's give him oxygen and get a large-bore cannula in,' Ben said sharply, breaking off momentarily as Ellie slipped quietly into the room.

For a brief moment their eyes met and he saw faint colour touch her cheeks. He gritted his teeth and forced himself to concentrate on his patient.

'Will, send bloods for U and E, FBC and blood sugar and cross-match four units. Ellie, can you run through some Haemaccel and we'll get that up while we're waiting for the blood. I want to do a femoral nerve block and then get this leg in traction.' He turned to the patient who was groaning in agony. 'Mike, I'm going to start by getting rid of that pain for you. I'm going to give you an injection into your nerve which will deaden the pain. It will just take a minute and then you'll feel better. Hang on in there.'

Carefully he palpated the femoral artery and inserted a 21-gauge needle, checking that he hadn't punctured a blood vessel before injecting the anaesthetic.

'All right, Mike.' Ben was still talking calmly to the patient. 'We're going to apply traction to your leg as quickly as possible because that will reduce the pain and the amount of blood that you're losing. It will also make it easier to move you while we take some X-rays. Ellie? Can you get a Donway traction splint, please?'

There was much activity and once the splint was in place Ben relaxed slightly.

'OK, folks, he fell from a height and that can be associated with a hip dislocation, pelvic fracture or fracture of the patella. I don't want to miss anything here so I want X-rays of the pelvis, hip and knee and the shaft of the femur. Ellie, can you bleep the orthopaedic reg, please?'

Ellie checked the pulse in the foot again and then hurried over to the phone.

Finally they transferred Mr Richards to X-Ray and Ben and Ellie were left alone in the room.

Immediately she hurried over to him, her eyes concerned. 'Are you OK?'

He stared down at her, totally thrown by her generous nature. Only a few hours earlier he'd told her that their relationship wasn't going anywhere, and here she was worrying about *him*. Didn't the woman ever think of herself?

He was still racked with guilt about the night before. 'Ellie listen, about last night…' He closed his eyes briefly. 'Did I hurt you?'

She blinked and then blushed prettily when she realised what he meant. 'No.' She shook her head and gave him a shy smile. 'It was fantastic, Ben. I just never knew it could—I could— Oh, help.' This time she looked away and he fought the temptation to drag her into his arms and repeat the experience on the hospital trolley lying vacant next to them.

No wonder his self-control had snapped.

Any man confronted with a woman like Ellie would have lost control.

He was stunned that she'd never made love before. *And he hadn't even noticed...*

'I should have taken more time.'

'Ben, why are you beating yourself up about this?' She touched him gently on the arm. 'In case you didn't notice, I was with you all the way. I wanted it as much as you did. There's no need to feel guilty, or apologise or worry about what you're going to say to me.'

He looked at her warily and voiced the question that was worrying him. 'Are we still going to be able to work together?'

'Of course we are!' She looked at him in amazement and then gave a delicious giggle that was pure Ellie. 'Unless you're afraid I'll rip your clothes off in public, and I have to say that there's a very high risk of that happening. It is my turn to undress you, after all. Talking of which, you owe me a new cardigan, Dr MacAllister!'

And new panties.

Remembering just how rough he'd been with her, he bit back a groan. How could he have behaved like that, and how could she joke about it?

She swiftly cleared the room around them and then strolled back over to him, her eyes mischievous.

'Ben, if you're still worrying about last night, please, don't. There isn't a woman in the world that wouldn't want a man to be so desperate for her that he tears her clothes to get to her body. Believe me, if I didn't have those sorts of fantasies about you before, it was only due to ignorance. But I'm not ignorant or innocent any more, and from now on I'll be having them all the time.'

Ben blinked, but before he could speak she walked over to him and stood on tiptoe to kiss his cheek.

'If you need a shoulder because you feel down, you know where I am, and if you need anything else...' she gave him a saucy wink '...you know where I am for that, too.'

With that she strolled towards the swing doors, casting a final look over her shoulder. But it was a look that heated his blood to a dangerous level.

CHAPTER NINE

IT WAS later in the afternoon when the doors crashed open and a burly, muscular man stormed into the department, clearly in a dangerous mood.

'Hey, you!' He marched up to Ellie and grabbed her arm, his fingers digging hard into her arm. 'I'm looking for Tina Williams and the kid. And don't tell me that they weren't brought in here, because I know they were.'

Ellie's heart dropped into her stomach. This must be Ken, Fiona's father. And she could see instantly why Tina was so afraid of him.

He looked like a bully and he acted like a bully.

'If you give me her details, I can check our records and see whether she's been in or not,' she said quietly, noticing that he smelt of alcohol.

'Don't mess with me, girl!' His fingers tightened on her arm and he jerked her closer to him. 'I want to know where she is, and I want to know if she's called the cops. There's a car outside. Is it for me?'

Ellie swallowed hard, completely out of her depth. 'If you let me go, I'll see what I can find out,' she repeated, working hard to keep the tremor out of her voice.

Why didn't someone come?

The corridor was normally heaving with people but now, just when she really needed someone, it was empty.

Intercepting her anxious look, Ken Foggarty gave a threatening growl and wrapped a muscular arm around her neck.

'They do know I'm here, don't they?'

Ellie gave a gasp and ripped at his arm with her hands. 'Let me go!'

'No way.' His arm tightened and for a frightening moment she struggled to breathe. 'I'm going to get what I want, and they're not going to stop me. Not if they want you alive.'

He looked around him, searching for something, and then he saw the double doors that led to the Resus room and gave a grunt of satisfaction.

Slamming a hand over her mouth, he dragged her bodily into Resus and flung her roughly across the room.

Caught off balance, Ellie smacked her head against a metal trolley and the world went black.

Five minutes later a white-faced Sean flung open the door of the small theatre where Ben was stitching a nasty laceration.

'I need to speak to you.'

Ben glanced at the wound. 'I've nearly finished here—'

'Now.'

Knowing his friend well enough to recognise that something was seriously wrong, Ben rose to his feet and made his excuses to his patient.

Outside he closed the door behind him and raised an eyebrow. 'Well?'

Sean licked dry lips. 'It's Ellie…'

'What about Ellie?' Looking into his friend's eyes, Ben felt a chill descend on him. He was seeing something in Sean's eyes that he'd never seen before.

Fear.

What the hell was he afraid of?

Sean closed his eyes briefly. 'Ken Foggarty has taken her hostage.'

It took a moment for the words to sink in and when they did Ben assumed he hadn't heard correctly.

'*Hostage?*'

'The police reckon that he saw the police cars outside and panicked. He obviously managed to walk into the department without anyone seeing him and grabbed Ellie—he's barricaded himself in Resus and he's using her as a bargaining tool.'

'For what?'

'He wants to see his partner.'

Ben considered the implications of that statement and closed his eyes briefly.

Remembering what Tina Williams had said about the man she lived with, he knew that the situation was serious.

Which meant that this time Ellie was in big trouble.

Ben could hardly breathe. Dear God, Ellie. His Ellie. Smiling, laughing, giving Ellie.

Ellie who thought that everyone could be trusted.

He ripped off his sterile gloves and started down the corridor but Sean put out a hand and stopped him in his tracks.

'There's something else you ought to know before you go rushing in there like a hero.' He released his hold on Ben's arm and rubbed a hand over the back of his neck. 'He has a gun. And the police think he won't hesitate to use it.'

Ellie opened her eyes and found herself staring at the gun.

She blinked twice and tried to remember everything that had happened. One minute she'd been in the corridor talking to Ken Foggarty and then he'd pushed her into Resus and she'd banged her head...

She closed her eyes and gave a low groan.

How on earth had she managed to get herself in this position?

Ben was going to be furious.

Her head was throbbing and she had no idea how long she'd been lying unconscious on the floor.

Had it been minutes or hours?

Did anyone know where she was?

She tried to lift a hand to her head and then realised that they were tied behind her back.

Panicking, she tugged at the ropes but they merely dug deeper into her wrists. She sagged back down onto the floor in frustration, realising that her ankles were tied, too.

How on earth was she going to get out of this?

'So—you've woken up, have you?'

Ken strolled towards her, his expression ugly, but all Ellie could see was the gun in his hand.

Maybe it wasn't loaded, she thought hopefully. Either way, there was no benefit in panicking.

'How long are you planning to keep me here?'

He fingered the gun. 'Until I get what I want.'

'And what's that?'

He frowned slightly, as if surprised by her calm response. 'She has to stop messing around and come back to me.'

Ellie stared at him. 'I assume you're talking about Tina. Is that what this is all about? Revenge?'

He shook his head. 'No, lady. Not revenge. This is good old-fashioned blackmail. Either she comes back to me, or I kill you. It's that simple.'

Ellie stared at him in disbelief. He was standing there like a madman, waving a gun around, and he expected Tina to come running home? She knew that there was no way that would happen. Tina was afraid of him.

'So you kidnapped me because you think that will make your wife love you?'

Having said it out loud, maybe he'd realise how ridiculous it sounded. If she hadn't been so scared she would have laughed. The man had a strange line in seduction techniques!

'I know she loves me.'

'Mr Foggarty—Ken—have you really thought this through? This really isn't the best way to make her come back to you.'

'She'll come back.' He was ominously calm. 'If she doesn't, I'll kill you.'

She looked at him closely and then shook her head. 'You wouldn't do that. I just know you wouldn't. You're just feeling very hurt and angry for some reason. I know that you're too nice a person to hurt me.'

His face darkened with anger. 'You don't know anything about me, lady!'

'As you said yourself, Tina loves you,' Ellie pointed out, 'which means that you must be a nice person. Just a bit mixed up, I suppose.'

'Just shut up!' He waved the gun angrily in her direction. 'I've had enough of your talking!'

Still watching the gun and wondering whether it was loaded, she tried to think rationally.

What should she do?

What exactly had Tina told her about him? She'd definitely said that Ken had changed since the birth of the baby.

So maybe the child was the key to how he was feeling.

'You haven't asked me how your little girl is,' she said, trying to keep her tone conversational. 'I looked after her when she came in.'

'I don't care about the kid. I just want my woman.' He glared at her and his hand tightened on the gun. 'Now stop talking!'

'She was very badly injured—'

'Then she shouldn't have come between me and Tina.'

So it was definitely the baby.

Ellie nodded sympathetically. 'Babies can be hard work, can't they?'

Ken's eyes narrowed, his breathing rapid. 'I told you to stop talking!'

'My cousin's just had one,' she told him, trying to ignore the feel of the rope biting into her wrists. 'She's always exhausted and she has much less time for Paul—that's her husband. It's very difficult.'

'That's enough—' he growled threateningly, but she ignored him and carried on talking.

'Becoming a family takes a lot of getting used to.'

'I don't want to get used to it! Now, for the last time, *shut up*!'

'All right.' Ellie's tone was patient and kind. 'But you're certainly not the first man to have problems adjusting to being a father. It might help just to talk about how you feel. It might stop you feeling so angry and confused. It isn't good to bottle things up and sometimes it's easier to talk to a stranger.'

His face turned red with anger. 'I don't need to talk! And if you don't shut up right now, I'll use this gun!'

She flinched at his tone and rolled her eyes. What was it about men? Why could they never talk about their feelings?

Ben was pacing up and down Sean's office like a caged lion.

He'd sent Will to finish off suturing the man in Theatre and he'd resisted the impulse to storm into Resus and rescue Ellie.

As Sean had rightly pointed out, that sort of behaviour could result in disaster. But it had been twenty minutes since Ken Foggarty had dragged her into Resus and no one seemed to be doing anything.

Jack Morgan marched into Sean's office moments later. 'What's happening?'

Sean's face was strained. 'The police have spoken to him on the extension in Resus and he wants to see his wife. They're dealing with it now.'

Jack let out a long breath. 'Right.'

'There's nothing right about it!' Ben slammed his fist against the wall, frustration and worry eroding his usual cool. 'There must be something more we can do to get her out of there.'

There was a long, tense silence and Sean shot him a curious look.

'Calm down, MacAllister. I've never seen you this worked up about anything before.' His gaze was suddenly sharply perceptive. 'Are you going to tell us why?'

Ben's jaw clenched. 'Because she's just a kid and she's probably frightened out of her wits.'

'And?' Sean didn't break eye contact and Ben gave a sigh as he was forced to voice what he'd only just realised himself.

'And because I love her.'

Seth gave a slow nod and a ghost of a smile crossed his features. 'For a highly intelligent guy, it took you a hell of a long time to work that one out, didn't it?'

Ben glared at him. 'I don't need one of your lectures.'

'Be quiet, the pair of you!' Jack rubbed his jaw, clearly thinking hard. 'I think you're all underestimating Ellie. I've never seen her frightened in my life and she's a bright girl. She'll find a way out of this.'

'That's exactly what I'm afraid of.' Ben gave a groan and rubbed a hand across his face. 'Knowing Ellie, she'll try and talk to him.'

Ellie sat on the floor of Resus, one eye kept warily on the man who was now sprawled on the floor next to her.

Despite the gun, she felt very sorry for him.

His life was a mess. And in his own way he clearly loved Tina.

'You know, if your relationship with Tina worked once, then maybe it can work again,' she said gently, bracing herself for another tirade of abuse.

He didn't answer.

Encouraged that he hadn't bitten her head off or waved the gun at her, she took a deep breath and carried on. 'She still loves you, Ken, but she's scared of you. And frankly I can see why. You clearly have a problem with anger. But you're not the first person to suffer from that. There are courses you can go on, you know.'

He scowled at her and his fingers tightened on the gun. 'I thought I told you to shut up—'

'You did, but someone needs to talk some sense into you,' Ellie said indignantly. 'The way things are at the moment, even if Tina agrees to come back to you, it will only be to help me and you don't want that. You want her to come back to you for good—because she wants to. Not because she's scared or threatened.'

He scrambled to his feet, his expression threatening. 'And what do you know about it?!'

'Not much,' Ellie admitted, 'but I do know that threatening to shoot me isn't going to help anything. You men are all the same. You're hopeless at talking about how you feel. Have you ever told her that you're jealous of the baby?'

His jaw tightened. 'I'm not jealous of the baby!'

'Calm down. It really doesn't matter if you are,' she said soothingly. 'Plenty of men feel that way, Ken. Having a baby is a huge adjustment. Massive.'

He was still clutching the gun, but there was a flicker of uncertainty in his eyes.

'Come on, Ken,' she urged gently, 'it's just you and me in here. Tell me how you feel. Give it a try.'

There was a long silence and then his shoulders sagged slightly. 'Before the baby came it was just me and her—' He broke off, clearly awkward about expressing his feelings.

'And after Fiona was born, Tina didn't have time for you any more,' Ellie finished softly, her expression sympathetic. 'You're not the first person this has happened to, Ken. Relationships change when babies arrive. But you need to talk about it. Tell Tina how you feel. You need to make time for the two of you.'

'I've never been much of a talker.' He glanced uncertainly towards the door. 'I don't know if I can start now...'

'Of course you can,' Ellie said firmly. 'You just did. You told me how you were feeling. A bit briefly maybe, but it was a start.'

He shifted slightly. 'It isn't that I didn't want a baby...' He cleared his throat awkwardly. 'It's just that it came as a shock. And everything changed. *She* changed.'

'I can imagine.' Ellie shared an understanding smile with him. 'If it's any consolation, it's perfectly normal to feel that way. There are people you can talk to about it, but the most important person to talk to is Tina.'

He lowered the gun and looked at her doubtfully. 'She'll never talk to me now.'

'I'm sure she will. Once you explain everything that you're feeling. She just didn't understand. It's pretty hard for us women to read men's minds.'

He rubbed a hand over his jaw. 'Is the baby going to die?'

'No.' Ellie shook her head. 'She was badly injured and she'll be in Intensive Care for a while, but they think she'll be fine.'

Thanks to Ben.

'Tina won't forgive me.'

'She loves you,' Ellie said gently. 'There's nothing that you can't forgive if you love someone.'

His eyes drifted to the nasty gash on her head. 'Does that hurt?'

'Not really. My fault entirely.' She managed a smile. 'I should have looked before I fell.'

The phone shrilled and he stiffened and tightened the grip on the gun.

'Put the gun down and pick up the phone, Ken,' she urged softly. 'And tell them that you want to talk to the police. Tell them what you've told me. And then we can get you to see Tina. Let's finish this before it gets any worse.'

He hesitated for a few seconds and then picked up the receiver.

'He's giving himself up.'

Ben stared at the policeman, hardly daring to believe him, but then he saw the door of Resus swing open and suddenly he knew it was true.

Without sparing the bulky man a second glance, Ben shouldered his way into Resus, his eyes frantically searching the room.

Was Ellie hurt?

Relief flooded through his veins as he saw her, bruised and bleeding but very much alive.

'Can you untie me? My wrists are killing me!'

She sounded so normal that he almost groaned aloud with relief.

In seconds he was on his knees beside her, the sharp blade of his knife slicing through the ropes that held her captive.

'Where's Ken?'

Ken? She was on first-name terms with her kidnapper?

'He's gone with the police.'

Ellie rubbed at her wrists and winced slightly. 'Well, I hope they're nice to him. The poor man is in such a state.'

He stared at her incredulously. 'Ellie, how can you call him a "poor man"? He kidnapped you at gunpoint!'

'I know, but it wasn't really his fault,' she said kindly. 'He was desperate, you see. He felt a lot better when we'd talked about it. That was why he gave himself up.'

Ben sat back on his heels and stared at her in disbelief. 'You talked him into giving himself up?'

'Well, it was his decision, of course,' she told him, 'but we talked it through together quite a bit.'

Ben blinked. 'You *talked it through*?'

'Of course.' She looked at him as if it was an odd question. 'He didn't want to at first. But he was obviously mixed up and tense so I chatted a bit to try and relax him and get him to open up—'

'Oh, Ellie…' Ben gave a groan and closed his eyes briefly. 'And what was his reaction to that?'

'Well, at first he threatened to shoot me if I didn't stop talking!' Ellie looked affronted and a glimmer of a smile crossed Ben's face.

'I'm sure he would never have kidnapped you if he'd known what you were like.'

'I just thought it would help if he talked about it,' Ellie said, and Ben shook his head, his eyes alight with humour.

'Presumably you told him that?'

'Of course!' She looked surprised at the question and Ben let out a long breath.

'In that case, it's no wonder he threatened to shoot you.'

'Nonsense. He needed to talk to someone and in the end he opened up quite a lot.' Ellie frowned thoughtfully. 'Well, I suppose I actually did most of the talking…'

'You astonish me,' Ben said dryly, his face darkening

with anger as he saw the blue-black bruise on her right eye and the blood on her cheek. 'Did he hit you?'

'Oh, no.' Ellie lifted a hand and touched her head. 'This was my fault. He let go of me suddenly and I hit the trolley. Tell me something, why is it that men have such trouble talking about how they feel?'

'Blame it on the tough, macho thing,' Ben said, his eyes still on her head as Sean and Jack hurried up to them.

'Everything OK here?'

It was now that he knew she was all right.

He scooped her up in his arms and laid her on the trolley so that he could take a closer look at her.

He still couldn't believe that she was alive. Alive and talking. Anyone else would have been totally floored by their ordeal, but Ellie was chatting away to the policeman now, explaining why he had to be tolerant to Ken.

She saw good in everyone.

Once the policeman had finished talking to her, she glanced at Ben cautiously.

'I suppose you're angry because I've got myself in trouble again.'

Her bravery squeezed his heart but he kept his tone light-hearted. 'Furious. And now I need to take a proper look at that head of yours. Were you knocked out?'

There was no way he was letting her out of his sight again.

Sean strolled up to them. 'That's nasty. Do you want me to stitch it?'

'I'll do it,' Ben said immediately, 'but she was knocked out so I suppose she ought to be admitted for observation.'

'No!' Ellie looked at him in horror. 'I don't want to stay in.'

Ben ignored her plea, moving his fingers gently over her temple as he examined her.

'Ouch!' Her face was pale and ghostly and he could see that she was in pain.

He picked up a torch, checked her eyes and carried on examining her, aware of Sean and Jack hovering next to him.

Finally he was satisfied that he'd checked everything. 'You'll live,' he said gruffly, wishing that the others would make themselves scarce.

There was so much he wanted to say to her, but not with an audience.

'I don't need stitches,' she said in a small voice. 'I just want to go home and take care of Max.'

'Ellie, you can't go home yet,' he reminded her gently. 'You need stitches. After that we'll talk about whether you can go home or not.'

Ellie sat in the A and E department, feeling utterly miserable. They wanted to admit her for one night's observation but the only place she wanted to spend the night was at home.

It was quite ridiculous. They'd sorted out her head and apart from a throbbing pain she felt fine. There was absolutely no reason for her to be in hospital.

Ben had gone to sort out a bed for her and she stared thoughtfully at the half-open curtain.

Dare she?

Without wasting any more time, she hopped off the trolley.

Peeping around the curtain, she saw that the corridor was empty and quickly tiptoed towards Reception. Heather looked up in surprise.

'Aren't you supposed to be resting?'

Ellie gave her a bright smile. 'I'm going home—can you call me a taxi?'

Heather hesitated and then nodded. 'All right. Hang on there a sec. I'll give them a call.'

Ellie hovered nervously, wishing that the taxi would come. Ben would be back any minute and he'd be furious if he caught her.

'I'll wait by the door,' she told Heather finally, edging towards the entrance of A and E, but unfortunately her exit was well and truly blocked.

The first thing she saw was a pair of powerful legs and then, as she gritted her teeth and forced herself to look upwards, she clashed with a pair of furious dark eyes.

'Where the hell do you think you're going?'

She flinched at his tone. 'Home?'

Her voice was little more than a guilty squeak and Ben glared at her. 'You were knocked out, Ellie. You need to stay in for observation.'

'I'll observe myself at home,' she suggested feebly. 'If I'm worried, I'll readmit myself.'

There was a commotion behind them and Sean strode up, his face black.

'What's going on?'

'She's being her usual reckless self,' Ben said abruptly, and Ellie felt her eyes fill.

Damn.

'I just want to go home…'

There was a long silence and then finally Ben spoke.

'All right, I'll take you home.'

Ellie gave a gasp of delight and Ben lifted a hand. 'On one condition.'

Ellie subsided. 'Don't tell me, I mustn't talk and I mustn't ask you any awkward questions.'

Sean looked baffled but a glimmer of a smile touched Ben's firm mouth. 'Actually, I was going to say that if I'm at all worried about you, you agree to go back to hospital.'

'Done.'

Sean frowned. 'No way, MacAllister. She lives on
her own—'

'Not any more she doesn't.'

Ellie's heart lurched in her chest but as usual Ben's expression gave nothing away.

Sean was still reluctant to let her go. 'She should be in
hospital.'

'You know her as well as I do.' Ben's tone was weary.
'Either I take her home or she'll make a run for it in the
night or do something equally reckless.'

Sean scowled. 'You promise not to let her out of your
sight tonight?'

Ben gave a short laugh and looked at Ellie. 'I promise
not to let her out of my sight ever again.'

Ellie's breathing was temporarily suspended.

What did he mean by that?

She peeped at him cautiously but he was still looking
at Sean.

'By the way, I need to take some holiday…'

Sean blinked. 'Right. When will you be back?'

'When Ellie's well enough to work. And when we've
had time to sort a few things out.' Ben reached into his
pocket for his car keys. 'I'm going to bring the car round.
Keep an eye on her until I get back.'

Ellie sat in silence in the car, staring straight ahead.

'Ellie, are you feeling ill?'

Ben's sudden question made her jump and she glanced
at him with a wan smile.

'No. Just thinking.'

'In that case, I'm seriously worried.' His tone was dry
and she looked at him in surprise.

'Why's that?'

'Because you never usually have a thought in your brain
that doesn't come out of your mouth,' he drawled, his

strong hands gripping the steering-wheel as he turned the car up the rough track that led to the cabins. 'You took such a risk in there, especially after he threatened to shoot you. I can't believe that even a gun couldn't keep you quiet!'

'I have serious trouble keeping quiet,' she confessed in a small voice, 'especially when I see someone bottling up his emotions. But maybe you're right. In future I'll take a vow of silence. Talking seems to get me into all sorts of trouble.'

'Well, I think perhaps it saved you tonight,' he said quietly, a glimmer of a smile touching his mouth as he pulled up outside the cabins. 'Do you have any idea how I felt when I found out he was holding you hostage?'

'Angry with me, I expect.' She risked a glance at him and her eyes widened as she saw the tortured expression on his face.

'Ellie, I wasn't angry. I was terrified.' Ben's voice was rough. 'I know what you're like. I knew that there was no way you'd keep your mouth shut. I was so afraid that you'd antagonise him.'

'Hey, I'm not stupid!' Ellie scowled at him but her scowl faltered as she looked into his eyes and saw the expression there.

'No, you're not stupid.' He touched her cheek with a gentle finger. 'You're the most loving, cheerful, optimistic person I've ever met, and you don't see bad in anyone.'

Her heart missed a beat. 'And I drive you crazy?'

There was laughter in his eyes. 'Completely.'

He walked round to her side of the car and scooped her into his arms.

His dark jaw was only inches away from her lips and the urge to kiss him was almost overwhelming.

'I could probably walk,' she said breathlessly, and he

gave her a look that she couldn't interpret as he opened the door to her cabin and carried her across to the sofa.

'Ellie, there are some things I need to say to you…'

'Oh.' Her heart sank. 'You're going to tell me off. Ben, you don't need to. I know I was a fool. I know that you're always having to rescue me. I owe you a huge debt—'

'That's not true.' He shook his head slowly. 'This time you rescued yourself, but if I have to rescue you every day for the rest of our lives, your debt to me will only be a fraction of mine to you.'

Breathing was suddenly incredibly difficult. 'Wh-what do you mean?'

'My life had been torture for so long,' he told her hoarsely, 'that I'd forgotten what it was like to feel pleasure, to experience anything other than pain and guilt. The way I dealt with it was to shut out the whole world. And then I met you and you refused to be shut out.'

Her heart was beating erratically. 'Ben…'

'And you wouldn't let me hide.' He took her hand in his, stroking her fingers gently. 'You wouldn't let me hide myself, and you wouldn't let me hide my pain. You were so loving and generous and in return you asked nothing. Nothing at all.'

She swallowed hard. 'Because I love you.'

His eyes locked with hers. 'I know that now,' he said softly. 'And I know that I love you, too. And I'm about to kiss you, so you'd better decide whether you're going to keep your eyes open or not.'

It was some considerable time later when he finally lifted his head. 'You closed them.'

'I know.' Her voice was shaky. 'I think I fainted. Can we try it again?'

The smile he gave her was so sexy that she felt her limbs start to tremble. 'Do you want to?'

'They say practice makes perfect…'

'Well, in that case, you have nothing to worry about,' he said softly, 'because you're going to get all the practice you need.'

She stared at him, heart thumping. 'I am?'

'Definitely. But before you agree to marry me you'd better understand that there are ground rules.'

The room spun round.

'Ground rules?' Her voice was a pathetic squeak and he gave a slight smile.

'Oh, yes, definitely ground rules.' Laughter lit up his dark eyes. 'Number one, absolutely no thumbing lifts. I don't want you climbing into cars with strangers.'

'No lifts.' Ellie stared at him, breathless. 'And number two?'

'Number two.' His fingers were still stroking hers. 'Number two, absolutely no stripping off in front of strangers. And no kissing strangers, with your eyes open or closed, no matter how good-looking they are. Even out of gratitude.'

'That's more than one rule,' she pointed out, and he scowled at her.

'I haven't finished yet.'

Her heart felt incredibly light. 'There's more?'

'Oh, yes.' His eyes dropped to her mouth. 'I can't stop you being reckless because that's part of your nature but no one, absolutely no one is to rescue you from your disasters apart from me. Understood?'

She nodded, smiling through her tears, and Ben lifted a hand to touch her damp cheek.

'You're the one who rescued me, Ellie. I never thought I'd be able to feel again, but I was wrong. You taught me to deal with my emotions. Do you remember that morning after we made love, you told me that I wasn't God? That I couldn't save every child?'

She held her breath, aware that he was finally talking

about his feelings and understanding just how difficult that was for him.

'Well, I suddenly realised that you were right.' His expression was serious. 'For two years I'd blamed myself for Hannah's death, believing that I should have been able to save her, but you made me see the truth. That no one would have been able to save her. You were right, and I was wrong. In fact, you were right about a lot of things. Like the fact that talking sometimes helps.'

They were both silent for a long moment and then he inhaled deeply. 'Marry me, Ellie, then I can spend the rest of my life making sure that you breathe between sentences.'

She gave a watery smile. 'I'll drive you crazy.'

'Very probably.'

'I'll get into scrapes.'

His smile was confident. 'Without doubt.'

'So how do you know it will work?'

His dark eyes gleamed. 'I've got one of my feelings…'

LIVE THE EMOTION

Modern Romance™
...seduction and
passion guaranteed

Tender Romance™
...love affairs that
last a lifetime

Medical Romance™
...medical drama
on the pulse

Historical Romance™
...rich, vivid and
passionate

Sensual Romance™
...sassy, sexy and
seductive

Blaze Romance™
...the temperature's
rising

27 new titles every month.

Live the emotion

MILLS & BOON®

MB3

MILLS & BOON®

Medical Romance™

THE SURGEON'S SECOND CHANCE
by Meredith Webber

Harry had loved Steph when they were medical students – but she married Martin. Now Steph is a widow – and Harry is back in town…and back in love! Harry knows he and Steph should be together, and he's not going to miss his second chance. He has to prove that she can trust him. But it won't be easy…

SAVING DR COOPER *by Jennifer Taylor*

A&E registrar Dr Heather Cooper isn't looking for love. But when she crosses paths with a daring firefighter she's frightened by the strength of her emotions. Ross Tanner isn't afraid of danger. To him, life is too short not to live it to the full – and he's determined to show Heather that his love for her is too precious to ignore.

EMERGENCY: DECEPTION *by Lucy Clark*

Natasha Forest's first day as A&E registrar at Geelong General Hospital held more than medical trauma. She came face to face with the husband she had thought dead for seven years! A&E director Dr Brenton Worthington was equally stunned. Somebody had lied, and Brenton needs to discover the truth!

On sale 6th June 2003

Available at most branches of WH Smith, Tesco, Martins, Borders, Eason, Sainsbury's and all good paperback bookshops.

0503/03a

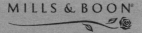

Medical Romance™

THE PREGNANT POLICE SURGEON
by Abigail Gordon

GP and local police surgeon Dr Imogen Rossiter is
fiery, beautiful – and pregnant! When she meets
fellow GP and police surgeon Dr Blair Nesbitt sparks
fly between them…until Imogen tells him she is
carrying another man's child. Both are thrown into an
emotional turmoil that tests the strength of their love.

THE GPs' WEDDING *by Barbara Hart*

Dr Fabian Drumm and Dr Holly Westwood were
happily planning their wedding – until Fabian's mother
told him his real father was not the man he called
'Dad' and he had half-siblings in America! Fabian
changes his mind about marriage and children – but
Holly refuses to give him up!

HER ITALIAN DOCTOR *by Jean Evans*

Dr Beth Bryant is determined to find fault with her
new boss – until she recognises him as the drop-dead
gorgeous Italian she saw that morning on her way to
work! Dr Nick D'Angelo spells sex appeal in the
extreme, and his romantic intentions are glaring. But
Beth doesn't want to feel the emotions of loving and
losing again…

On sale 6th June 2003

*Available at most branches of WH Smith,
Tesco, Martins, Borders, Eason, Sainsbury's
and all good paperback bookshops.*

0503/03b

MILLS & BOON

Summer of
LOVE

CANDY HALLIDAY

HOLLY JACOBS

CATHIE LINZ

ELISE TITLE

Available from 16th May 2003

*Available at most branches of WH Smith,
Tesco, Martins, Borders, Eason, Sainsbury's
and all good paperback bookshops.*

0603/49/MB75

Don't miss *Book Ten* of this BRAND-NEW 12 book collection 'Bachelor Auction'.

On sale 6th June

Available at most branches of WH Smith, Tesco, Martins, Borders, Eason, Sainsbury's, and all good paperback bookshops.

BA/RTL/10

0503/73/MB73

MILLS & BOON

DON'T MISS...

MILLS & BOON

BETTY NEELS

THE PROMISE OF HAPPINESS
& CAROLINE'S WATERLOO

THE ULTIMATE COLLECTION

VOLUME ELEVEN

On sale 2nd May 2003

Available at most branches of WH Smith, Tesco, Martins, Borders,
Eason, Sainsbury's and all good paperback bookshops.

MillsandBoon.co.uk

books | authors | online reads | magazine | membership

Visit millsandboon.co.uk and discover your one-stop shop for romance!

Find out everything you want to know about romance novels in one place. Read about and buy our novels online anytime you want.

✱ Choose and buy books from an extensive selection of Mills & Boon® titles.

✱ Enjoy top authors and *New York Times* best-selling authors – from Penny Jordan and Miranda Lee to Sandra Marton and Nicola Cornick!

✱ Take advantage of our amazing **FREE** book offers.

✱ In our Authors' area find titles currently available from all your favourite authors.

✱ Get hooked on one of our fabulous online reads, with new chapters updated weekly.

✱ Check out the fascinating articles in our magazine section.

Visit us online at
www.millsandboon.co.uk

…you'll want to come back again and again!!

WEB/MB

2 Books
and a surprise gift!

We would like to take this opportunity to thank you for reading this Mills & Boon® book by offering you the chance to take TWO more specially selected titles from the Medical Romance™ series absolutely FREE! We're also making this offer to introduce you to the benefits of the Reader Service™—

- ★ FREE home delivery
- ★ FREE gifts and competitions
- ★ FREE monthly Newsletter
- ★ Books available before they're in the shops
- ★ Exclusive Reader Service discount

Accepting these FREE books and gift places you under no obligation to buy; you may cancel at any time, even after receiving your free shipment. Simply complete your details below and return the entire page to the address below. *You don't even need a stamp!*

YES! Please send me 2 free Medical Romance books and a surprise gift. I understand that unless you hear from me, I will receive 4 superb new titles every month for just £2.60 each, postage and packing free. I am under no obligation to purchase any books and may cancel my subscription at any time. The free books and gift will be mine to keep in any case.

M3ZEB

Ms/Mrs/Miss/Mr ....Initials..
BLOCK CAPITALS PLEASE

Surname..

Address..

....

....Postcode ....

Send this whole page to:
UK: The Reader Service, FREEPOST CN81, Croydon, CR9 3WZ
EIRE: The Reader Service, PO Box 4546, Kilcock, County Kildare (stamp required)

Offer not valid to current Reader Service subscribers to this series. We reserve the right to refuse an application and applicants must be aged 18 years or over. Only one application per household. Terms and prices subject to change without notice. Offer expires 29th August 2003. As a result of this application, you may receive offers from Harlequin Mills & Boon and other carefully selected companies. If you would prefer not to share in this opportunity please write to The Data Manager at the address above.

Mills & Boon® is a registered trademark owned by Harlequin Mills & Boon Limited.
Medical Romance™ is being used as a trademark.